Dea~
th~
have a ~
open too!

Love Penny
2015

STORIES FOR
8 YEAR OLDS

A Random House book
Published by Random House Australia Pty Ltd
Level 3, 100 Pacific Highway, North Sydney NSW 2060
www.randomhouse.com.au

First published by Random House Australia in 2014

Text copyright © see acknowledgements for individual stories
Illustrations © Tom Jellett 2014

The moral rights of the authors and the illustrator have been asserted.

Addresses for companies within the Random House Group can be found
at www.randomhouse.com.au/offices

National Library of Australia
Cataloguing-in-Publication Entry

Title: Stories for eight year olds/edited by Linsay Knight
ISBN: 978 0 85798 475 3 (pbk)
Target audience: For primary school age.
Subject: Children's stories
Other authors/contributors:
  Knight, Linsay, editor
  Jellett, Tom, illustrator
Dewey number: A823.01089282

Cover illustration by Tom Jellett
Cover design by Leanne Beattie
Internal design and typesetting by Midland Typesetters, Australia
Printed in Australia by Griffin Press, an accredited ISO AS/NZS
14001:2004 Environmental Management System printer

Random House Australia uses papers that are natural, renewable and
recyclable products and made from wood grown in sustainable forests.
The logging and manufacturing processes are expected to conform to the
environmental regulations of the country of origin.

STORIES FOR 8 YEAR OLDS

Stories by
**R.A. SPRATT, PAUL JENNINGS,
ALEESAH DARLISON AND MORE!**

Edited by
LINSAY KNIGHT

Illustrated by
TOM JELLETT

RANDOM HOUSE AUSTRALIA

FOREWORD

BACK BY POPULAR DEMAND!

What a treat it is to search for the special stories that tickle children's tastebuds and find a treasured place on their burgeoning reading menus, to be sampled again and again. This collection showcases these stories in order to excite eight-year-old readers, enable them to test their growing skills and continue their reading adventure in a safe and reassuring environment. And that's why we have also given such careful consideration to the reading requirements of this age group, such as content, author style and voice, as well as the ratio of text to illustration and type size.

    With growing confidence and feeling increasingly comfortable with fewer illustrations and smaller type, these readers are eager to try out their skills on a range of different genres. They feel at home with a whole range of storytelling styles, including folk and fairy tales, often with a wicked twist at the end. Adventure stories and humorous tales that extend personal experience to invoke unfamiliar worlds can be explored. As always, Tom Jellett's black-line illustrations are used to provide added meaning to the text and to help speed up and slow down the action when the plot requires heaps of excitement or pause for thought.

The third of four specially selected collections, *Stories for 8 Year Olds* includes offerings from the following inspirational Australian storytellers: Aleesah Darlison, Bill Condon, C. N. Archer, Claire Craig, George Ivanoff, Jane Jolly, Lizzie Horne, R. A. Spratt, Sally Gould and Paul Jennings.

We are proud to present such a friendly and accessible book, essential for children who adore being read to and demand a good read.

– Linsay Knight

CONTENTS

A DIFFERENT SORT OF KELPIE

BY ALEESAH DARLISON

'Who knows what a kelpie is?' Mr McDougall asked the class one morning.

Hands shot up. We lived in Yass, sheep country. Everyone knew what kelpies were.

'They're working dogs,' I said. 'They're rusty-red with green eyes.'

'Or black and tan,' Will added.

'They have pointed ears and pointed faces,' Holly said. 'We've got three. My dad reckons they're the backbone of Australia.'

Mr McDougall laughed. 'I see you know what Australian kelpie dogs are. Has anyone ever heard of a different sort of kelpie?'

Everyone shook their heads.

'The kelpie I'm talking about comes from Scotland, where I grew up,' Mr McDougall said. 'It's also called a water horse.'

Will's face scrunched. 'What's a water horse?'

'Like in that movie,' Holly said. 'The Loch Ness monster.'

'That's another type of water horse altogether,' Mr McDougall said. 'A bigger one that lives only in lakes. Those water horses are also called *Ech-Ushkya*.'

'*Ech-Ushkya*?' Will's face scrunched again.

Mr McDougall nodded. 'The water horse I mean is much smaller and only lives in rivers.'

'There's no such thing as water horses,' Sam said. 'Just like there's no such thing as bunyips.'

'Believe me, kelpies do exist,' Mr McDougall said. 'I used to own one. Shall I tell you about it?'

'Yes, please!' we all said.

Mr McDougall leaned back in his chair. 'I was twelve when I saw my first kelpie. We lived on a sheep farm in north-west Scotland. My mum died when I was little so it was just Dad and me. We didn't have much money so I had to help Dad on the farm after school and on the weekends. It was hard work, but I enjoyed it.

'Now, kelpies are well known in Scottish legend. Dad often told me stories about them. That they live in the deepest, darkest depths of the river and only come out at night or early morning when the fog lies thick all round. That sometimes they appear in semi-human form, with long, mangy hair covering their body and seaweed for hair.'

'Gross,' Holly said.

'Yes, not pretty,' Mr McDougall nodded. 'In this form, the kelpie hides and waits for a passing traveller, then leaps up and crushes them to death in its strong arms or chases them until it grows tired of the game

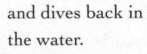

and dives back in the water.

'Other times, the kelpie appears as a magnificent horse wearing a bridle. Anyone silly enough to mount it will be taken for a ride they'll never escape from.'

'How come?' I asked.

'The kelpie's shaggy coat sticks stronger than glue,' Mr McDougall explained. 'Once the rider's on, they can't get off. The kelpie dives back into the water, taking the rider with it and drowning them. Some legends say kelpies lure children to eat for dinner.'

'What about your kelpie?' I asked. 'Did you ride it?'

'I'm getting to that,' Mr McDougall said. 'One year, Dad got sick and had to go to hospital. Every day after school I caught the bus to visit him. When the bus dropped me home one afternoon, I noticed lightning flashing in the distance. A storm was coming. As I passed the river near our farmhouse, I heard a strange wailing sound that made the hairs on the back of my neck prickle.

'I stared out across the river to where the wailing was coming from.

The water frothed and churned and I saw a horse galloping on the surface. I was so frightened I raced home, locked the doors and windows, jumped into bed still wearing my rained-on clothes and pulled the covers over my head. My teeth were chattering and my body was shaking with cold and fear.

'As I huddled there while the storm growled overhead, an idea struck me. Dad once told me that, if caught, a kelpie was a valuable animal to have. It could do the work of ten land horses. I thought if I caught the kelpie we could use it on the farm.

'I knew it was a dangerous and stupid thing to do, but I had to try. I checked in the stables and found an old bridle. I headed to the river and waited for hours in the rain. There was no sign of the kelpie.

'Eventually, I gave up and went home. The next night, I searched for the kelpie again. Nothing. For five nights, I kept a lookout without any luck. I thought about giving up. Dad was due home from hospital soon and there was no way he'd let me go out looking for the kelpie once he was back. I had to try one more time.

'On the sixth night, I went to the river and waited. I was so tired I could hardly keep my eyes open. I must have fallen asleep because I remember being woken by the sound of rain. I looked up and saw something glinting on the water. It was the kelpie's eyes, just above the surface. I stayed in my hiding spot in the heather. My heart was pounding so loudly I thought for sure the kelpie would hear it. Slowly, it began to rise up out of the water until –'

'Was it the hairy seaweed creature?' Holly asked.

'No. It was a black horse as dark as midnight and dripping wet with strands of seaweed in its mane. The kelpie trotted onto the riverbank and started eating grass. I crept towards it. Even in the darkness, I could see it was strong and muscular.'

'Weren't you afraid?' Will asked.

'Absolutely,' Mr McDougall laughed. 'I knew if my plan didn't work, I'd end up at the bottom of the river. But I kept thinking how marvellous it would be to own such a fine horse. Anyway, I held my hand out to the kelpie, talking softly to it. I told it that it was the most beautiful creature I'd ever seen, the strongest, the sleekest, the most powerful.

'The kelpie nickered, enticing me to come closer. All the while, I held the bridle behind my back. I knew I had to mount it and get my bridle on quickly or else the creature's magic would overcome me and I'd be stuck.

'Still talking, I inched closer and then leapt onto the kelpie's back. Its coat was glossy like a seal, smooth and cold as snow to touch. The kelpie whinnied. I felt myself becoming stuck to the kelpie's wet coat already. Trying not to panic, I slipped the kelpie's bridle off and put mine on. When the kelpie realised I'd switched bridles, it was furious. It raced along the riverbank, squealing and bucking. I thought I might fall off, but its glue-like coat held me firm. After a while, it calmed down. The spell was broken. The kelpie was mine.

'As the sun came up, I trotted home.
I settled the kelpie into the stable and gave it
cornmeal to eat. The next day, I rode it into
town. That kelpie was fast, I can tell you!
When my dad walked out of hospital and
saw it, he knew straight away it was a kelpie.
No matter how hard I rubbed the kelpie
down, its mane always dripped with water.'

'Did you use the kelpie on the farm?'
I asked.

'Yes,' Mr McDougall said. 'That animal
did do the work of ten horses. Over the
years, the kelpie and I grew very fond of
each other. Of course, I could never take the
bridle off. The kelpie's magic would have
returned and it would have tried to trick me,
even though I took good care of it.

'Years passed. I finished school and had
to leave home for college. Dad was old by
then. He decided to sell the farm and move

to the city with me. We couldn't just leave
the kelpie. Nor could we sell it or take it
with us. So, late one night I took it back
to the river.

'When I got there, I patted the kelpie
one last time and thanked it for everything.
Carefully, so I didn't touch its coat, I
removed my bridle and slipped the one it
had been wearing when I'd caught it back
on. The kelpie nickered as if to say goodbye,
then trotted into the river.

'I never saw it again. But the day Dad
and I left, a storm blew over the moors and I
heard that same sad, eerie wailing I'd heard
years ago when I saw my kelpie for the first
time. It still made the hairs on the back of
my neck prickle.'

As Mr McDougall's story ended, the
class sat silently, letting his words fold
around them.

'That's an awesome story,' Will said.

'Thanks, Will,' Mr McDougall said.
'Now, class, I've told you a story. How about
you each write one for me?'

'Does it have to be a true story?' I asked.

'That's up to you,' Mr McDougall said.
'The important thing is that you make me
believe.'

THE BIG BAD BAH!
BY BILL CONDON

CHAPTER ONE

Mum and Dad gathered all the family around to tell them something really important.

'I've heard a few of you talking about what you want to do when you grow up,' Mum said.

My six brothers and sisters nodded enthusiastically.

'I want to be a dancer,' said Gypsy, jumping high and spinning in the air.

'And I want to be a great and famous soccer player,' I said.

'I'm sure all of you would be good at whatever you decided to do,' said Mum. 'However, there is one small problem.'

'What?' asked Gypsy.

'There's no easy way to break this to you.' Mum took a deep breath. 'You're all . . . dogs.'

'Dogs?' Jasper gasped. 'But I was going to be prime minister!'

'No! No!' cried Carmen. 'I was going to be a dentist!'

'It's impossible!' snapped Tulip, who'd had her heart set on being a mountain climber.

'Sorry,' said Dad. 'It's true.'

Oscar rolled over and played dead.

'Does this mean I can't be an actor?' asked Minnie.

'Not at all.' Mum smiled. 'There have been many famous dog actors.'

'They can earn lots of money,' added Dad.

'Do dogs earn lots of money playing soccer?' I asked.

Dad shook his head. 'Most dogs love chasing balls, Sasso, but they don't play soccer professionally.'

That was bad news, but even worse was to come . . .

Two weeks later, Mum and Dad gathered us together once again.

'Unfortunately,' Mum began, 'our masters, Louise and Thelma, can't afford to keep nine dogs.'

'We were expecting this,' Dad said. 'It happens all the time to dog families.'

'Expecting what?' Gypsy asked.

'Louise and Thelma want your dad and me to stay with them,' Mum said, 'and they can also keep Oscar and Carmen. But I'm afraid the rest of you puppies will have to find new homes.'

OH NO!

CHAPTER TWO

We howled and we whimpered until Dad's warning growl made us stop.

'Come now,' he told us, 'you're behaving like a bunch of kittens.'

The next day a small van came to pick us up. It had the words DOG POUND written on it.

'What does "dog pound" mean?' Minnie asked.

'It's a place where really special dogs go,' Mum said. 'They'll look after you there – I promise.'

Hearing that made us all feel a lot better. For a moment I thought we were being packed off to the unwanted dogs' home, but no, we were *special*.

Louise and Thelma were sorry to see us go. 'Are you sure they'll all find good homes?' they asked the van driver.

'Pretty sure,' the driver said. 'They're all nice-looking puppies.'

Dad puffed his chest out proudly. 'I think they got their good looks from me,' he told Mum.

'No, dear,' she replied. 'They got their fleas from you – the good looks were all from me.'

We all laughed, even Dad. And then it was time to leave.

Mum and Dad gave us a mushy lick, and Carmen and Oscar barked their goodbyes. We were sad, but at the same time we also knew we were about to start a great adventure. It was exciting!

CHAPTER THREE

Everyone was friendly at the dog pound. We were washed and brushed until not a single hair was out of place.

'Why are they making such a fuss over us?' Minnie asked.

Gypsy knew. 'It's because people are coming to look at us today. If we're lucky they might give us a new home.'

Just then a gate squeaked open and a group of people walked into the yard. My sisters and brother stood up close to the gate doing their best to look cute as the humans came close.

Gypsy danced.

Tulip climbed on top of her kennel.

Minnie rolled over on her back so her belly could be tickled.

And Jasper wagged his tail so hard I thought it might come right off.

I was too shy to do any of those things. Instead, I stayed back inside the kennel.

'I'll take this one, please,' said a lady as she picked up Gypsy and cuddled her.

'This one's for me,' said the man who'd been tickling Minnie's tummy.

A young girl pointed to Jasper and Tulip. 'These ones for me!'

I put my head outside the kennel so she could see me.

'I'm over here,' I said. 'Take me!'

She didn't even look at me. One by one my siblings licked me goodbye.

For the first time I was a little bit worried.

CHAPTER FOUR

Over the next two weeks people came to the pound nearly every day. Each time, another dog would push me out of the way and be chosen instead of me. I took a good hard look at my reflection in a puddle. I wasn't very good-looking at all.

'Who would choose me?' I mumbled aloud.

'Plenty would! If you take a few tips from me.'

It was the voice of Tiger, the cocker spaniel in the kennel next to me. Tiger was only in the kennel as a visitor. He liked to jump his owner's fence and go for long walks. Every time, the dogcatcher brought him to the dog pound, and every time his faithful owner took him back home. He was an expert on people.

'I'd really appreciate any advice you could give me, Tiger,' I said.

'Okay, Sasso. First thing you do is look lively. Humans want a dog, not a turtle.'

'You mean I should hop about and bark?'

'Hop, yes. Bark, no! Only bark *after* they've fallen in love with you.'

'Do you really think they'll fall in love with me?'

'For sure! Here come some humans now.'

'I'm scared, Tiger.'

'Don't be. Here's a tip that never fails . . .'

I leaned closer.

'Chase your tail!'

'My tail? But that's silly.'

Tiger winked. 'Trust me.'

Next moment two humans were patting me.

'I'm not so sure,' said the lady named Daisy. 'This one is a bit too quiet.'

'There's plenty of others to choose from,' said the man called Paul.

Tiger growled. 'The tail! The tail!'

I felt ridiculous, but I did it. Around and around I circled, chasing my tail.

'Look!' said Paul.

'How cute!' Daisy picked me up and stroked me. 'On second thoughts,' she said. 'I like this little puppy.'

CHAPTER FIVE

My new home was great. It had lots of grass for me to romp around in. Plenty of toys. And three meals a day.

I even had a friend to play with – Amber, the labrador who lived next door.

'You're lucky to have Daisy and Paul looking after you,' Amber said. 'They're kind people.'

'I don't know much about people,' I admitted.

'They're complicated,' Amber said. 'Just make sure you let them know that you're the boss.'

'How do I do that?'

'Listen closely,' said Amber.

For the next two hours Amber shared her secrets. By the time I'd finished that bone, I was a different dog.

The next time Paul or Daisy opened the back door – *zoom!* – I was into the house and resting on the lounge before they knew it.

When they took me walking I dragged them along so fast they almost fell over.

I also tore out every plant in the garden. But I didn't touch a single weed!

And it was just like Amber said it would be – no matter how bad I was, Daisy and Paul forgave me.

'I'm proud of you,' said Amber. 'You've proven you're in charge. Now, if I were you, I'd stop while I was ahead.'

'No way! I'm having too much fun.'

The next day I ripped all the washing off the line.

Then I chewed up the hose.

'I think you're making a big mistake,' Amber said.

'No, I'm not. They love me. I can get away with anything,'

One day a truck pulled up out front. It had a sign on it that said, DEANO THE DOG TRAINER.

CHAPTER SIX

'What's your puppy been up to?' asked Deano.

Daisy and Paul produced a long list of complaints.

'I'll soon teach her to behave,' said smartypants Deano.

Just to prove how wrong he was, I snatched one of Paul's slippers and ran with it around the yard. Yee-ha!

'BAH!'

It was like a cannon exploding in my ears. I dropped the slipper and ran away.

Next, Deano opened the back door and called my name. I came bounding over, willing to forgive and forget.

As soon as I started barging inside the house, he threw a chain against the door.

CRASH!

At the same instant, he yelled, 'Bah!'

I'd never been so scared! I ran out of the house as fast as I could.

'A dog's hearing is fourteen times more sensitive than a human's, said Deano. 'When Sasso is naughty, throw down the chain and say "Bah". She'll soon mend her ways.'

That night Daisy and Paul walked me around the park. Every time I started pulling him along, Paul roared, 'Bah!'

When I tried biting the lead in half, Daisy threw the chain down at my feet. *Bah! Crash! Bah! Crash!*

It was too much for any dog to take. They'd won.

CHAPTER SEVEN

As soon as I got home I rushed over to Amber so I could tell her about my terrible day.

'I told you not to go too far,' she scolded.

'But what can I do now, Amber? The "Bah" is awful. Throwing the chain down is even worse.'

'Calm down, Sasso. I can help you get used to loud noise.'

'How?'

'My humans have a teenage son called Jack,' Amber said. 'When his parents aren't home he plays heavy metal.'

That night I sat with Amber outside Jack's window as he played crashing and banging music for hours.

After listening to the music every night for a week, even the loudest thunder didn't worry me at all.

Now to try my luck with the chain.

I slipped inside the house and made myself comfortable on Daisy's favourite chair.

'Sasso, get off my chair,' she ordered. 'If you don't, I'll throw down the chain.'

I pressed the recliner button and stretched out full-length.

Crash! Crash! Crash!

Daisy was red in the face from throwing the chain, but I hardly even noticed it.

'Paul! Sasso won't get off my chair. Throwing the chain doesn't work anymore.'

'I'll soon fix her,' said Paul. 'BAH!'

'Ouch!' It was the biggest bah I'd ever heard. It was much louder than Jack's music. I ran for my life.

Paul went for one last mighty 'Bah' but, instead, a croaking sound came out.

'Are you all right?' Daisy asked.

'I think I've hurt my throat,' he muttered. 'I've done too much *BAH*-ing.'

'Dogs rule!' I cried.

CHAPTER EIGHT

Now I knew exactly what to do. I hopped onto Daisy's bed.

'Bah!' she yelled.

I barked while she was watching her favourite TV show.

'Bah!'

I howled at the full moon.

'Bah! Bah!'

In the morning Daisy held her throat and whispered, 'Paul, I can hardly talk.'

'Me too,' he croaked back.

There was no doubt about it now – I was the boss!

But then Daisy started crying and Paul held her in his arms.

'All I wanted was for us to be a happy family,' she sobbed. 'But Sasso only makes me sad.'

I felt really bad. They didn't deserve this, not after being so good to me. The more Daisy cried, the worse I felt. I wasn't a dog. I was a dirty, rotten rat!

Right then and there I made up my mind to change my ways.

I wagged my tail as hard as I could, and I gave them both a big wet lick on the nose. They spluttered and pulled faces, but I knew they liked it.

'Oh, so you're being a good dog now, are you?' said Daisy.

I nodded and put my paw up for her to shake hands.

'If only you could be like that all the time,' Paul said.

'I can,' I barked. 'Just give me a chance.'

I sat at their feet and looked up at them with adoring eyes — and there wasn't even any food around!

'You know what?' Daisy patted me on the head. 'I've got a feeling that Sasso understands what's going on.'

I licked her hand to let her know she was right.

Ever since that day I've been on my best behaviour.

Now life is so good.

No more throwing down chains.

No more yelling *Bah!*

And Daisy and Paul are happy because they have the perfect pup.

Hey, that's me!

At last, I have a family again.

HERBERT HUFFINGTON: TEA-LEAF READER EXTRAORDINAIRE

BY C. N. ARCHER

Herbert Huffington had never suffered the misfortune of being popular, ordinary or lucky. But what can you expect when you're a lime-green three-foot-tall dragon with purple freckles trickling down your back?

Herbert lived in the quiet town of Wallowmarsh Lane, where he ran a tea store on the corner of Third and Main Street.

This was quite fortunate as the townsfolk of Wallowmarsh Lane happened to consume more tea per square metre than any other town in the entire world.

Herbert was a sensible dragon, as far as dragons go. He wasn't involved in any type of jewel-stealing or sheep-eating behaviour and he made a concerted effort to fit in. For example, it wasn't unusual for him to stroll about town with his thirteen Persian cats, dressed in a tweed suit and balancing a tousled toupee on his head.

You would assume that, in a town filled with guzzling tea-lovers, a world-renowned tea expert would

be quite popular. Alas, Herbert was not.
You see, whenever the dragon became
excited, nervous or anxious he would
sneeze. For you or me, this quirky habit
would be nothing more than a snotty
nuisance. But as everyone knows, when
a dragon sneezes, red-hot flames burst from
its nostrils.

This became a little bit of a problem.

When Beatrice Butterworth, the mayor's
eight-year-old daughter, complimented
Herbert on the colour of his freckles, he
sneezed and burnt down the dentist surgery.
And when Herbert's tea won first prize
at Wallowmarsh Lane's Royal Show, his
excited sneeze set fire to the town hall.
These incidents, however, were minor
compared to what happened when Herbert
decided to dabble in the mystical art of
tea-leaf reading.

On the morning of the Wallowmarsh Lane Parade, at precisely ten o'clock, Herbert unlocked his store. He turned around the 'open' sign and brewed his first pot of tea for the day. Sunday's blend was always Russian Caravan, one of Herbert's favourites, and its aroma was pleasant to everyone but toads and camels.

Herbert took out the book he'd just borrowed from the library: *Fortune Flavours – A Beginner's Guide to the Art of Tea-Leaf Reading*. He skipped straight to the chapter on fortune-telling, then skimmed over the small print at the top of the page.

Inappropriate use of tea-leaf reading can result in dire and life-threatening consequences. Do not attempt to use tea-leaf reading to interfere with, or change, the future. Never, ever read your own fortune. Caution: steaming hot tea can burn and scald the mouth.

As it turned out, the rather fascinating and mystical art of tea-leaf reading was neither difficult nor complicated.

Step 1. Make a lovely cup of tea and drink it, making sure there are plenty of tea leaves left in the bottom.

Step 2. Squint at the cup (with one eye, or both, depending on your personal preference).

Step 3. The leaves will twirl into images of the future.

Herbert was quietly confident he could easily handle the first step in the process. But before he could try his hand at it, the bell above the front door jingled and Beatrice Butterworth strode into the store. She wore a pale pink dress with a crimson coat and matching shoes.

'Good morning, Beatrice. Happy Parade Day!' Herbert smoothed down his toupee.

'Happy Parade Day to you as well, Herbert.' Beatrice smiled as she peered at the tins of tea on the long metal shelves. 'My father would like some of your raspberry, rhubarb and rosemary blend.'

Herbert clapped his hands and smiled. 'Oh, yes. A rather delicate but delightful drop of tea. It'll take just a moment to prepare. Can I offer you a cup of Russian Caravan while you wait?'

Beatrice nodded. 'That would be lovely.'

Herbert selected his fanciest cup and poured Beatrice a generous slurp of tea. While he measured out the correct quantities of raspberry, rhubarb and rosemary, Beatrice sipped her tea and browsed the store.

Herbert packaged the tea mix, throwing a complimentary packet of shortbread biscuits into the bag. 'Here you go.'

'Thank you very much!' Beatrice handed Herbert her empty teacup and left the store in a whirl of smiles.

Herbert waited until the door closed behind her before he peered into Beatrice's cup. He examined the swirls of tea leaves and discovered that, at exactly 4 pm, Beatrice would win a sixteen-layer cream-filled strawberry sponge cake in the raffle at the local bakery. He also saw that at 4.05 pm she would trip in the middle of Main Street and squish her prize into a flat, strawberry-sponge mess.

Herbert's brow furrowed and he shook his head. 'There must be something I can do,' he muttered to himself. A smile crept upon his face as the most marvellous idea occurred to him. 'I could stop Beatrice from tripping and then her cake wouldn't be ruined!'

Herbert shuffled his feet in a gleeful dance. A ball of fire burst from his nose and rolled down the centre of the store.

'Oops!' Herbert blushed and covered his nostrils with his tiny hands.

The front door jingled, followed by a flurry of customers. They demanded tea, tea and more tea. Herbert was so busy serving his customers all day, he hardly thought about his plan.

At 3.57 pm he glanced at the clock and squawked. Despite their protests, he ushered out the remaining customers and hurried to the bakery. He waited under a tall willow tree out the front of the local greengrocer.

Herbert smiled and greeted the townsfolk as they scurried past him. Some replied but most scuttled out of the way, giving the little fire-sneezing dragon a wide berth.

Trevor Tibbles, the greengrocer, rushed out of his store to stand between Herbert and the mango display he'd spent three hours arranging. 'Uh, hello, Herbert. Why don't you stand on the other side of Main Street? Um . . . there's far more shade and a lolly –'

'Happy Parade Day, Trevor!' Herbert stepped forward and shook his hand. 'No, thanks, I'm waiting for someone.'

Trevor sighed and muttered something about chargrilled mangoes.

A cheer erupted from within the bakery and a moment later Beatrice appeared. She was carrying the sixteen-layer cream-filled strawberry sponge cake. She stepped onto the road, the cake wobbling from side to side.

'Let me help you with that,' said Herbert, jumping out from behind the bush with a big smile on his face.

Herbert's sudden appearance startled Beatrice. She squealed and tripped over, falling on top of the cake. Sponge and strawberries splattered all over her beautiful dress and whipped cream covered her hair.

'I'm so sorry, I didn't mean to scare you!' Herbert's face turned bright red and he shuffled backwards, smoke billowing from his nostrils.

Trevor ran forward to help, but slipped on a stray piece of sponge and landed next to Beatrice with a thud.

Herbert clenched his nostrils as he attempted to resist the overwhelming urge to sneeze. 'A . . . ah . . . ahhhh . . . Ah-choooo!'

A stream of fire spurted from Herbert's nostrils and into the willow tree. The thin, leafy branches burst into flames. The force of the sneeze hurled Herbert into the mango stand. Hundreds of mangoes rolled into

Main Street. Meanwhile the parade, led by Mayor Butterworth and the town's marching band, turned the corner of Second Street and commenced their walk down Main Street.

The first mango rolled past Mayor Butterworth without too many problems. The second bounced with more purpose and struck him on his left knee. Mayor Butterworth tumbled backwards, knocking over the poor trumpet player behind him. The trumpet player fell on the saxophone player. The saxophone player bumped the flautist. The entire marching band tumbled over like a row of dominoes.

The townsfolk gasped. All eyes followed the path of destruction, which led back to Herbert.

'You've ruined Parade Day, Herbert!' the mayor bellowed from amongst the jumble of musical instruments and band members. He shook his fist in the air. 'You ruin everything!'

A single tear welled in Herbert's eye. He turned and ran back to his tea store as fast as his little legs could carry him. He slammed the front door and stomped upstairs to his apartment, slumping into a faded blue armchair. His thirteen cats surrounded him, some leapt on his lap while others rubbed up against his legs and tail. A chorus of purring echoed around the room.

'Well, tea-leaf reading didn't go as well as expected.' Herbert's shoulders drooped. 'Mayor Butterworth is angry. I'm afraid we might need to move away from Wallowmarsh Lane.'

The cats tilted their heads and meowed at Herbert before slinking into the kitchen. They returned dragging and pushing a portable blackboard. The largest cat dropped a piece of chalk at the dragon's feet.

'You're right. I can fix this!' Herbert picked up the chalk and brainstormed ideas.

At 10.43 pm Herbert finally stepped back to examine his work. In the centre of the board he'd scribbled 'Good Deeds' with arrows running to the names of various townsfolk and all manner of suggestions. Herbert circled 'Beatrice = Cake', 'Mayor = Tree' and 'Trevor = Mangoes'.

Herbert nodded to the cats. The cats nodded back.

Herbert then set about preparing a sponge cake. But he'd never baked before and didn't have a cake recipe. Even worse, he didn't have any strawberries or cream in his refrigerator. This did not deter him. He did his best to fashion a cake out of flour, milk, canned tuna and black olives.

After letting the sticky (and rather stinky) mixture set, Herbert tiptoed out of the apartment with the olive tuna sponge cake in one hand and his bag of tools in the other.

The street lamps cast a large dragon-shaped shadow along the buildings as Herbert crept through town. He left the cake on Beatrice's porch with an apology note.

Next, he made his way over to the greengrocer's and searched for the mangoes. He finally found them out the back in crates. Herbert gently carried the bruised and battered fruit to

the front of the store and constructed an elaborate mango pyramid for Trevor.

Herbert then turned his attention to the smouldering trunk of the town's willow tree. He scratched his head and wiggled his nose until he spotted a rather lovely rosebush in Mayor Butterworth's front yard. Herbert proceeded to replant the rosebush in front of the former tree.

An exhausted but satisfied Herbert walked home. He was so tired, he didn't even go upstairs. Instead, he curled up into a ball and fell asleep in the middle of his tea store.

———

When Herbert woke the following morning, he felt rather optimistic about the success of his midnight good-deed-doings. He brewed a fresh pot of Monday's tea, English

Breakfast. After slurping all of his tea in one big gulp, he glanced at the tea leaves swishing around the bottom.

Herbert dropped the cup and squawked. He hadn't meant to, but amongst the leaves he'd read his own future. He'd seen an image of the townsfolk chasing him and his cats down Main Street.

Herbert raced upstairs and began shoving his belongings into a small suitcase. He explained the situation to his cats and they helped by sneaking as many cans of tuna into the suitcase as possible. Once he'd put harnesses on all thirteen cats, he led them downstairs and out onto Main Street.

'I know none of you are excited about moving to Antarctica, but apparently penguins and polar bears make wonderful companions.' Herbert shuffled as fast as he could while carrying a suitcase and dragging the leads of thirteen reluctant cats. 'Who doesn't love tea-flavoured ice-cones?'

'Herbert! Stop!'

As the little dragon and his cats reached Fourth Street, a mob of angry townsfolk appeared on Main Street.

'Wait!' Beatrice Butterworth ran ahead of the crowd until she caught up with Herbert. 'Where are you going?'

Herbert stopped and sighed. 'My cats and I are moving to Antarctica.'

'Why?' Beatrice asked as Mayor Butterworth appeared behind her. 'Won't you get eaten by a polar bear?'

Herbert's cats raised their fluffy eyebrows in alarm.

'Um, I don't think so. I believe they prefer to eat smaller animals like penguins and snow cats –' Herbert grimaced, glancing at his cats. 'No, it definitely should not be a problem.'

'We're sorry for getting angry yesterday. Everyone's come to apologise!' Beatrice gestured to the townsfolk before nudging her father in the ribs.

'Yes, I'm sorry for calling you names,' Mayor Butterworth whispered to Herbert. 'It was uncalled for and terribly rude.'

Beatrice coughed and glared at her father. 'Pardon? I couldn't quite hear you.'

Mayor Butterworth repeated himself so all the townsfolk could hear.

'And?' Beatrice tapped her foot.

'And we've appointed you as voluntary member of the town fire brigade, so if you sneeze you can put the fire out yourself!'

Herbert blushed and puffs of smoke popped out his nostrils. 'I don't know what to say. That would be fantastic!'

'Good! Now, you're going straight home and you'll forget all about this silly Antarctica business,' said Beatrice, yanking Herbert's suitcase out of his hands.

So, not only did Herbert and his cats stay in Wallowmarsh Lane for a very long time, but they became welcomed and loved. Herbert could often be found rescuing balloons snagged in the branches of tall trees and giving lectures on fire safety to the local scout group. And instead of strolling about town wearing his toupee, Herbert switched to his fire-fighter helmet which he found to be infinitely more stylish and comfortable.

HARRIET BRIGHT AND THE VERY BIG FRIGHT

BY CLAIRE CRAIG

KING OF THE STREET

'HEY, YOU! HARRIET BRIGHT!'

Harriet Bright felt her stomach slippery dip. Then it hit the side of her ribs.

Boing

She thought it was going to bounce right up out of her throat.

Oh no! Not now. She was so close to home.

She looked around quickly. The street was very quiet. It was the in-between time after school had ended and before people came home from work.

There was no one around.

Only a fat black cat.

Harriet Bright wished that it was a fierce jungle tiger snarling through the bush with its jaws wide open, its sharp teeth ready to attack, its roar echoing through the trees.

The black cat opened a lazy eye. Its silky fur glistened in a spotlight of sun. It closed its eye and curled up tight.

Harriet Bright kept walking.

Okay, pretend she hadn't heard. Only 783 steps to go and she'd be safe.

782

781

780

She could hear Paul Picklebottom. He was scuffing his shoes along the pavement.

He was far enough away at the moment.

But he was getting closer.

Harriet Bright's brain was alert. She was thinking. What should she do?

Plan A: Outsmart the enemy. Take a shortcut through Wiley's Creek, sneak through Mrs Pilchard's backyard and climb over the fence to home.

Disadvantage: Could end up in the creek. Again!

Plan B: Run fast. Screaming for HELP! Disadvantage: Loss of dignity. Forever.

Plan C: Think of Plan D.

721 steps

720

719

A POET, DON'T YOU KNOW IT

'I'M SPEAKING TO YOU . . . FATTY!'

Paul Picklebottom just had a way of saying that word.

He shouted the first syllable FAT and hissed the second through his teeth TY, like air escaping from a tyre.

Harriet Bright thought FATTY sounded square and solid. Just the shape she saw when she looked at her reflection in the window of Joyanne's Fashions on High Street.

Mrs Glossia, her English teacher, said there was a special name for words that sound like the thing they are:

ONOMATOPOEIA

Harriet Bright thought there were lots of words like this. Such as 'plump' (round and juicy), 'podgy' (stuffed with pastries and meat pies) and 'blob' (dollops of thick custard and cream).

Harriet Bright's mother said that she had puppy fat. 'You'll grow out of it,' she promised.

Harriet Bright had read that snakes shed their scaly skins when they got too big for them. She wondered when she would grow out of her lumpy skin.

She could hang it in the wardrobe.

For emergencies.

Like if she burnt herself rescuing a cat trapped in a house on fire.

Or she could use it later.

When her skin got old and tired.

She knew what was coming next.

HARRIET BRIGHT
WHAT A SIGHT!
LEGS LIKE JELLY
WITH A BIG
   WOBBLY
       BELLY

Snigger. Snigger.

Paul Picklebottom had taken months to come up with that. And all he could think of to rhyme with jelly was . . . BELLY!

Harriet Bright scoffed. He had no imagination. Not like her.

Mrs Glossia said that Harriet Bright's poetry was very 'individual'. She particularly liked Harriet Bright's space poem:

When I'm in space I feel so alone
and I am very sorry you cannot telephone.

I miss the movies and there aren't any shops,
and my friend is a giant called Cyclops.

Harriet Bright is going to be a poet when she grows up.

'HEY! FATTY BONANZA.'

As soon as Paul Picklebottom is out of her life.

612 steps

611

610

WISHING YOU WEREN'T HERE

Harriet Bright closed her eyes tight.

Her mother said that if you wished really hard for something and then counted to ten, it might just happen!

Weasels and sneezels and snails on toast
turn Paul Picklebottom into a ghost.

1 2 3 4 5 6 –

'FATTY BOMB-O-LA-TA! YOU LOOK LIKE A CHIP-O-LA-TA.'

Harriet Bright opened her eyes. Paul Picklebottom was laughing and pointing at her.

Maybe wishing only works in the morning, thought Harriet Bright.

Mrs Glossia said that morning was definitely the best time to think, because your brain was fresh.

Harriet Bright had seen pictures of a brain in a book. It looked like a tangle of raw sausages.

Paul Picklebottom had thought so too. He had snatched the book from her hands. 'Hey, sausage brain,' he had snorted. 'Your brain would be good for breakfast! With lots of onions on the side.'

533 steps

532

531

Harriet Bright wondered why short distances sometimes seemed so long.

She could see her yellow house with the red roof and the green fence, but her feet seemed to be moving extra slowly. Almost as if she hardly weighed a thing.

Mrs Glossia had told them all about gravity last Tuesday. She said that gravity kept everybody on the ground.

Not like in space.

Harriet Bright imagined she was

one of the first astronauts to land on the moon.

The moon was cold and silent. She stared at the blue earth below.

Millions of people watched on TV as Neil Armstrong – the most famous man in space – the first man to walk on the moon – held the door of the spacecraft open for her.

Harriet Bright was going to be the
First   Child   Girl
Nine-year-old poet
To walk on the moon.

Her body was a big balloon, light and floaty in her spacesuit as she took slow-motion steps across the bumpy ground.

Harriet Bright was just about to speak to the WORLD (she had written a special poem for the occasion) when –

'PUDDING FACE! TRY THIS ON FOR SIZE.'

A chocolate-coated doughnut with a huge bite out of it hit her on the head.

IN A PICKLE

Of all the planets in deep dark space
Paul Picklebottom isn't from the human race.
He's big and heavy and tall and mean.
He's a monster from Mars and his insides
are green!

The doughnut was sticky from the sun and the chocolate stuck in Harriet Bright's hair.

Harriet Bright really liked chocolate doughnuts.

But not today.

393 steps
392
391

Harriet Bright was getting very close to her house.

    387 steps
    386
    385

But Paul Picklebottom was getting very close to her.

She could hear his heavy footsteps behind her.

Harriet Bright was frightened.

It was just like feeling carsick.

Her father said that feeling carsick was a load of old rubbish. 'Mind over matter,' he said.

When Harriet Bright was sick all over the front seat of their new car on a trip to the coast last year, her mother said, 'It doesn't matter, darling.'

Her father slammed on the brakes and screamed, 'WET ONES!'

Then he glared at her. He *really* seemed to mind!

Harriet Bright's mother told her to think of something else when she felt sick.

Harriet Bright thought of all the words that rhymed with pickle:

stickle   fickle   nickel   tickle

She could only think of one word that rhymed with bottom, but it was a good one: **rotten**.

Harriet Bright wondered how the Picklebottoms got their name.

Maybe people who eat pickles get big bottoms, she thought.

There should be a warning on the pickle bottle.

No one at school teased Paul Picklebottom about his name.

No one at school teased him about anything.

He was too big.

Her mother said she should ignore Paul Picklebottom.

Her father said Paul Picklebottom should pick on someone his own size.

Paul Picklebottom said she was a 'double-sized elephant'.

ON THE RUN

Harriet Bright had read all about elephants.

She knew that they are the biggest animals on land and that there are two types, African and Asian.

Elephants can't see very well and they all live together in groups called herds. This means that they can protect the young elephants from dangerous animals that might attack them. Like lions and tigers.

And Paul Picklebottom.

She could hear him breathing. He was only about 20 steps away.

19

18

17

Harriet Bright closed her eyes. She imagined that she was in Africa.

Her skin felt dry and cracked in the burning sun. She filled her trunk greedily with water from the muddy waterhole, squirting it into her mouth and hosing her hot body.

Several hippos swam nearby. Large eyes bulged out of their heads and their heavy bodies disappeared into the murky water.

The air *twitched* with insects and all the smells of the animals mingled in the heat.

But there was another smell too.

Something that made the birds *squawk* and f l u t t e r high into the air.

Something that made the elephants TRUMPET and R O A R.

It was the smell of danger, snaking slowly across the ground.

12 steps
11
10

Harriet Bright could feel her trunk tingling.

Her senses were on standby.

Her brain was mission control.

Receiving. Loud and clear.

Danger ahead!

Attack!

'A A A R R R G G G H H H!' shouted Harriet Bright as she charged towards Paul Picklebottom with a herd of elephants following closely behind.

The ground pounded with furious footsteps and clouds of dust gathered around the storming animals.

Paul Picklebottom looked completely surprised.

He dropped his schoolbag and took off in a giant hurry, *screech*ing around the corner.

He didn't stop running till he had crossed Wiley's Creek, bolted through Mrs Pilchard's backyard and clambered over the fence into his home.

Harriet Bright watched him go.

When the dust settled, she kicked a little stone and began to dawdle the last few steps home.

She already had another poem in her head.

LIQUID MOUSE

BY GEORGE IVANOFF

Benjamin quickly hid himself behind the large scratching post in the corner of the office. Tentatively, he peered out from his hiding place and shivered.

A huge old cat had entered through the cat flap. His fur was dirty grey, his left whiskers were missing and a large scar ran over his permanently closed right eye. He looked like he had seen many a fight. In contrast, his suit was of the finest cut – undoubtedly a designer brand. Great Uncle Whiskers only ever wore the best. He casually lifted a paw, licked it and cleaned his remaining whiskers. Then he meowed his readiness to receive visitors. It was a deep, guttural sound that made Benjamin's tail twitch.

I must be crazy, Benjamin thought, as another cat entered. *I'm a mouse. I shouldn't be here, in the heart of the underground feline headquarters.*

But Benjamin had little choice. The cats had captured his brother, Franklin, and he was determined to rescue him. He pushed aside his dread as he listened to the cats.

'It's almost ready!' The Siamese cat that had entered looked nervous and quivery. His backwards baseball cap and cross-eyed gaze gave him a comical appearance. 'It just needs to be tested.'

'Excellent, my little Saki. Excellent!' Great Uncle Whiskers chuckled. 'There's worldwide interest in our little project, thanks to our website. Human technology certainly has its uses.' He chuckled again, and his good eye glazed over as his thoughts wandered. 'If only they knew. They think they're so smart, keeping our kind as pets. But these pets make excellent spies, stealing their secrets . . . learning their technology.' He looked back at Saki, his lips curling back in a sneer. Benjamin caught a brief glimpse of rotting teeth. 'And now we have put their technology to our own uses.'

Benjamin stifled a gasp. Cats weren't supposed to have human technology.

'The greatest invention the feline world has ever known.' Saki was very excited, his eyes darting from right to left. 'And it's all thanks to you.'

Great Uncle Whiskers nodded with satisfaction. 'Are we ready for the test?'

'Yes! Yes, we are!' Saki was bouncing on the spot with excitement. 'We captured a new batch of mice this morning.'

Benjamin's ears pricked up.

'I hope no one has eaten any.' Great Uncle Whiskers scowled. 'I don't want any delays in the testing. The sooner we have achieved Liquid Mouse, the better.'

Benjamin shuddered as the cats left. Liquid Mouse? He didn't know what it meant, but it didn't sound good. His brother was definitely in danger. Trembling from nose to tail, he crept out of hiding and followed the cats.

————

Great Uncle Whiskers and Saki disappeared through a cat flap with TOP SECRET printed across it. Benjamin crept up to the flap and carefully lifted a corner. The two cats were now with a third – a large

explosion of white fur squeezed into a lab
coat and wearing round wire spectacles.
All three were staring intently at a large
piece of machinery.

Benjamin snuck in and ducked behind
another scratching post. From there he was
able to inch further down the room, past
storage crates and a large tower of empty
glass bottles. He peered out from between
two boxes. The cat in the coat was smiling –
at least, Benjamin thought she was. It was
hard to tell – she had such a squashed in face.

'Magnificent! Magnificent!' Great Uncle Whiskers inspected the machinery. 'You've done well, Professor Gertrude.'

Benjamin gazed up at the machine. It was huge – at least four stretched cats in height, and six in width. It was a great mass of wires, gears and other mechanical bits and pieces. The row of pistons on the front looked like a menacing set of teeth, with two gauges above for eyes. It towered over Benjamin like some huge monster, ready to devour him. On one side, a conveyor belt led to a mouse-sized doorway with the word IN printed above. A clear tube with the word OUT hung from the other end.

'How does it work? How does it work?' Saki was springing up and down on the spot, his eyes gazing in opposite directions.

'Iz very simple,' The Professor indicated the doorway, with a flourish of her paw.

'Ze mice enter here.' She pointed to the tube at the other end. 'Once ze liquifying process is complete, ze Liquid Mouse comes out there – fresh and delicious, ready to be bottled. All ze leftover furry and crunchy bits are strained away – zey can be used for compost. Very environmentally friendly.'

Benjamin's eyes widened in horror.

Great Uncle Whiskers chuckled. 'It will take the feline world by storm.' He licked his lips and grinned, baring his rotting teeth. 'And at last I'll be able to savour the taste of mice again. It's been so long since I've been able to chew . . . and I'm sick of porridge.'

'Liquid Mouse! Liquid Mouse!' Saki was prancing about. 'Gonna bottle some Liquid Mouse!'

Great Uncle Whiskers cuffed him over the head, knocking his cap off. 'Enough! Go get the mice!'

Saki picked up his cap. 'Okay, boss.'
Then he raced out.

Benjamin looked around, frantically trying to think of a plan.

'Ze machine is controlled by zis computer.' Professor Gertrude was leading Great Uncle Whiskers to the other side of the machine.

The computer, thought Benjamin, *that's it.*

Benjamin made his way around the back of the grinning monster, never taking his eyes off it, in case it sprang to life. As the cats moved to the opposite side, he dashed over to the computer table. He shimmied up the leg and examined the back of the computer. There was a large cable leading from it to the machine. It was a very thick cable, and Benjamin didn't know what else to do but to . . . chew it. He just had to hope he could chew through it in time.

Benjamin was soon distracted by Saki bounding back through the cat flap. He was followed by ten mice, eyes downcast, wearing striped prison overalls. Coming up behind the mice were two more cats – each of them clutching a mouse trap pointed threateningly at their prisoners. They had several more traps attached to their belts.

The mouse at the head of the line glanced up briefly and caught Benjamin's eye as he peered around the computer. It was Franklin. He quickly returned his gaze to the floor so as not to give his brother away. Benjamin's heart skipped a beat.

Saki herded the mice towards the conveyor belt while the other two cats stayed by the flap, guarding against escape.

'Would you like to do ze honours, sir?' Professor Gertrude pointed to the computer.

Great Uncle Whiskers nodded and strode over.

'It's all set.' The Professor dashed to his side. 'Just double-click ze mouse on zat icon.'

'Mouse? What mouse?' Saki leapt up, eyes almost popping from his head. 'Has a mouse escaped?' He dashed over to the computer.

Great Uncle Whiskers cuffed him again. 'Just keep an eye on our test mice. We don't want them escaping.'

'Okay! Okay, boss!' Saki dashed back, hissed at the mice, then paced up and down beside them.

Great Uncle Whiskers slowly shook his head, then looked accusingly at Professor Gertrude. 'It's a *dog*, okay. We renamed it. Don't let me catch you using the human term for it again – especially not around Saki. Now, start this thing.'

Professor Gertrude nodded and double-clicked the dog.

Benjamin looked up as a low throbbing sound came from the machine. The monster was waking up. Slowly, gears and pistons began to move, lights began to flicker, and as their pace increased, a high-pitched grinding noise began. He gazed down at the cable – he wasn't even halfway through – then back at the machine. He would have to do something else.

He peered out from behind the computer. Saki had removed the chains and was herding the mice onto the conveyor belt. Franklin was at the head of the line. Panic-stricken, Benjamin edged his way around the side of the computer. Backing up against the monitor, he snaked his tail around it, aiming it at the keyboard. Reaching the *escape* key he pushed with all his might. But nothing happened. It was a large key and he wasn't strong enough.

'What's that?!' Great Uncle Whiskers was staring at Benjamin's quivering tail, hissing. 'We have an intruder! Guards!'

The two guards by the flap dashed across the room as Benjamin came out into the open. He was about to jump onto the *escape* key when both cats threw their mouse traps.

The first trap landed by the *escape* key, its metal clamp snapping down on the key  and cracking it in half. The second trap landed upside down and triggered, springing across the keyboard and smashing into the monitor screen. The resulting explosion catapulted Benjamin across the room, right into Saki. The astonished Siamese was knocked to the floor. Benjamin, whose fall had been cushioned by the cat, staggered to his feet, dazed. As his vision cleared, he saw that the whole place was in chaos.

The mice were jumping down from the now-stationary conveyor belt. The professor was twisting dials and pulling levers, trying to shut down the machine, which was now going crazy. It was making weird belching noises, showering sparks and billowing thick, purple smoke. Great Uncle Whiskers was hissing and spitting at the guards who were heading towards Benjamin.

'Run!' Benjamin cried out.

As the mice took off across the room, the guards started throwing more traps. One of the traps went off at the base of the tower of bottles, starting an avalanche of glass that crashed down onto the guards. A stray bottled hurtled into Saki, who was just getting to his feet, knocking him down again.

Great Uncle Whiskers fixed Benjamin with a one-eyed stare of loathing and stalked towards him. Benjamin raced for freedom. But just before he reached the flap, Great Uncle Whiskers pounced, pinning him to the floor. Holding him down with one paw, he raised the other and slowly extended its claws. As the paw started its downward sweep, Franklin and one of the other mice grabbed the edges of a primed trap and hauled it over behind the huge cat. Great Uncle Whiskers howled with pain and indignation, falling back, his tail caught in the trap. Benjamin was up and through the flap in seconds.

As the mice ran through the maze of sewers, Franklin turned to his brother.

'Thanks for getting us out of there. Now
we've got to get to a squeaker-phone and let
the United Mouse Technology Council know
about the liquifying machine.'

Hmmm, wondered Benjamin. *Perhaps
they could adapt the cats' idea.* He grinned.
Liquid Cat!

RAMS VS MAGPIES

BY JANE JOLLY

Sam jumped out of the ute and raced to the footy change rooms to meet Adam.

'Behave yourself,' called out Dad.

Sam grinned.

Today was the A-Grade semifinal between their team, the Ramlap Rams, and the Maroonda Magpies. It was a home game. The Rams had been the favourites to win until their star ruckman, big Nick Forrest, came down with the flu. He wouldn't be playing today.

'Hey, Adam,' called Sam.

'Whatcha doin'?' asked Adam.

'Dunno. Let's go.' The boys raced off around the oval.

The oval was right next to the showgrounds and the sheep and cattle yards. Today the sheep yards were full. That usually meant there was a sheep sale in the next day or so. There were hundreds of sheep in the pens and about twenty or more huge big-horned rams in another pen.

Adam picked up a stone and skimmed it across the backs of the sheep. They bleated and ran into the corner of the yards.

Sam laughed. 'Stupid sheep.'

The boys got to a tall pine tree. It was their favourite. They could climb up it and watch the game without being seen. They could also see what was going on underneath them without anyone knowing they were there.

Sam raced up the tree. Adam followed and soon they were perched right at the top. Just in time for the start of the game.

When the Rams ran onto the oval Sam and Adam cheered and hollered. Sam pulled a pine cone off the tree and threw it into the air. It fell to the ground and landed right in front of Toby Green.

'Oi! Who threw that?' he yelled.

Sam and Adam sat quietly. Toby was the town bully from Maroonda. Skinny with freckles and red hair, he was in Year Seven. And he had a gang. There was always trouble when he came to footy.

'Watch this,' Adam whispered to Sam. He pulled another pine cone off the tree and this time aimed it directly at Toby. It hit him right on the head.

'Hey!' yelled Toby.
He looked up at
the tree.

Adam made a
squawking sound like
a cockatoo and they both
waited. Toby looked up
again and then walked away.

'I'm starved,' said Sam.
'Let's get a pie.' The boys
shimmied down the
tree and, making
sure Toby was nowhere near, dashed out
and ran to the canteen. Sam's mum was on
duty and his sister Katie was helping her.
They had come in earlier in the day to
set up.

'Can we have a pie, Mum?' asked Sam.

'Two pies coming up,' said Katie.

The boys walked off, scoffing their pies.

Sauce dripped down their shirts. They had just walked around the corner when they heard, 'Hello, hello. What do we have here?' It was Toby. 'Got any money on you?'

'Get lost, Toby,' said Adam.

'I would if I could but I'm too clever to get lost,' sneered Toby.

'Come on, Adam. Let's go,' said Sam. He didn't want Adam stirring up Toby. The boys headed back around to the pine tree while Toby moved off into the crowd.

The match was very even. It was almost goal for goal. If the Rams didn't win today they would be out of the finals.

At three-quarter time the Rams were down by six points. Sam and Adam got down out of the tree to get a drink. Sam's mum gave them each a can of soft drink from the canteen.

They walked back around to the sheep yards and were looking at the rams when they heard a familiar voice.

'Got me a drink, did you? That was very nice of you.'

It was Toby and he was with two other boys. Sam could see there was no way out of this one, so he gently shook his can behind his back. Adam saw what Sam was doing and did the same with his.

Toby smiled. 'Pass them over and there won't be any trouble,' he said.

Sam handed his over to Toby, and one of the other boys grabbed Adam's can from him. Sam stepped back and waited. Toby tugged at the ring pull on his can and held it up to his mouth when he was hit in the face with an explosion of soda. It frothed and bubbled in a jet stream. The same thing was happening to the other boy. They both yelled out and threw the cans down. Their faces were dripping with soda.

'You're dead meat!' yelled Toby as he threw the can down.

Sam and Adam took off. They raced round the back of the sheep yards. Toby and his mates split up and chased after them. Soon Sam and Adam were cornered.

Sam jumped the fence into the sheep yards, Adam following close behind. The boys jumped from pen to pen, trying to get away from Toby and his gang. The sheep bleated and ran around in circles. They were packed in so tightly it was hard to move through them. Sam fell over a couple of times, landing in the dirt and getting a mouthful of sheep droppings.

The air was full of red dust and the stale smell of sheep wee. The boys coughed and spluttered as they tried to escape from the gang.

'You're a loser, Sam!' shouted Toby.

Sam jumped another fence. But this time, when he looked up he froze. A herd of rams stood and stared back at him.

'Hi . . . guys,' said Sam. One of the rams bleated. 'It's okay. Good boys. Nice boys.'

A huge ram in the corner stared at him, then lowered its head and charged at Sam as he ran to the gate.

'Look out!' called Adam.

Sam looked up and saw Toby standing in front of the gate. He was trapped. It was Toby or the ram. Sam flicked open the gate and ran. The huge ram ran out after him and all of the other rams followed. He heard Toby yell in astonishment as he raced screaming towards the oval.

Sam sprinted onto the oval, just as the last quarter of the footy match commenced, closely followed by the rams. The huge one still had its head down, ready to butt anyone or anything in its way.

People started jumping out of their cars to try to stop the rams. One old farmer chased after them, waving his hat and yelling. A man whistled at his kelpie, which had been sleeping in the back of their ute.

The umpire didn't know what to do. He just kept blowing his whistle. There were people and rams running everywhere. One of the Maroonda fullbacks got butted from behind and fell down screaming.

Sam ran to the scorer's box and climbed up the ladder. Old Bill was sitting there laughing his head off.

'What's the score, Bill?' asked Sam.

'Rams one, Maroonda nil,' said Bill.

Sam searched the oval for Adam but couldn't see him anywhere.

The kelpie from the ute ran out onto the oval and was trying to round up one of the rams. Ten other dogs joined it. They weren't sheepdogs, rather, it was a jumble of poodles, pugs, Jack Russells and even a massive husky. The dogs chased the rams and some chased each other.

People sitting in cars around the edge of the oval tooted their horns. Then the footy siren blew. As the players ran off the oval, a voice came over the loudspeaker asking everyone to get the dogs off the oval. Ben Cross, who was the local sheepdog breeder, went home and came back with three of his best dogs. The rams were soon rounded up and put back in the yards.

Sam snuck off back to the ute. As he went past the canteen he saw Toby Green. His mum was yelling at him. Toby had a rip in his pants and his shirt was stained with soft drink.

'Get in the car now!' ordered his mum. Toby hung his head and walked off.

Sam couldn't resist it. 'Hey, Toby! How's it going?' he yelled, before running off like a shot out of a gun.

He ran straight into Adam.

'What happened to you?' asked Sam.

'I got knocked over by one of the rams. Look!' Adam pointed to his mouth. It was bleeding and there was a space where he had lost a tooth.

'Wow! What's your mum going to say?' said Sam.

'She's already said it,' said Adam. 'She's okay. When I told her we were running away from Toby Green she started on about him and forgot all about me.'

'What about your tooth?' asked Sam.

'It's only a baby tooth,' said Adam.

'We lost the footy. That means we're out of the final,' said Sam.

'Yeah, I know,' said Adam. 'Uh-oh, here comes your dad. I'll see you later.'

Sam's dad strode up to Sam. 'Was that you, Sam Burns, who I just saw leading those rams onto the oval?' he asked.

'Yes,' mumbled Sam.

Before he could say anything else his dad grabbed him by the scruff of the shirt and said, 'Come with me, young fella.'

His dad marched him into the change rooms. The whole Ramlap Rams team was sitting silently on the benches.

'Here's our man. The one who let the rams out,' said Sam's dad. 'Samuel Burns.'

Sam stood with his head down. And then the whole team and all their supporters let out a huge cheer. Sam looked up. Everyone was laughing and slapping each other on the back. What was going on?

'What a champ,' said the captain. Sam looked over at his dad. He had a big grin on his face.

'The game has been cancelled and we get to play again next week. Nick will be better by then and we'll kick their pants,' said the coach. More cheers went up and Sam found himself being lifted up onto the players' shoulders.

They carried him around the change rooms and gave him three cheers. Then they began singing, 'Who let the rams out? Baa, baa, baa, baa. Who let the rams out? Baa, baa, baa, baa.'

They finally put Sam down and he and his dad made their way back to the ute. They passed the canteen where his mum and Katie were packing up.

'Hello, love,' smiled his mum. 'What can I get our champ?'

'Can I have a soda, please?'

'Another one?' she said.

'Yeah,' said Sam. 'I gave the other one away.'

THE MOBILE PHONE

BY LIZZIE HORNE

CHAPTER ONE

'Ben, this is Fergus,' said Mr Pringle.
'Fergus, meet Ben.'

'Hi!' said Ben in a friendly voice.

It was Ben's job to look after Fergus.
Fergus was from a school in the city that had
come to visit Ben's school in the country. He
was going to catch the school bus home with
Ben and stay at his house for two nights and
do everything that Ben normally did. It was
going to be so much fun. Even just walking

up the driveway was an adventure at Ben's place!

He put his hand out to a boy who was bigger than him, with smart shoes and shorts, a sharp haircut and a mobile phone in his hand.

But Fergus didn't put his hand out to Ben. He just shrugged and slung his backpack over one shoulder and poked at his mobile.

'Well . . . come on then,' said Ben. 'We have to go out the front to wait for the bus.'

Fergus nodded his head and followed.

'Do you get a bus home from school where you live?' asked Ben.

'Nah,' said Fergus.

Ben waited, but Fergus didn't tell him how he did get home from school. He didn't say anything; he just kept walking and fiddling with his phone.

Ben had thought of a million questions to ask Fergus about living in Sydney, but suddenly they all seemed stupid.

At the bus stop, lots of other children from Ben's class were chatting excitedly with their billets.

'On Tuesdays, after school, I go to ballet,' Angela was saying to her Sydney person, who was also named Angela.

'So do I!' said the other Angela. They linked little fingers and giggled.

'Wow! That must be amazing, catching an underground train home from school!' Rocky was saying to Lim.

Lim's chest puffed up. 'I've been allowed to get the train by myself since the middle of last year.'

'In the city! By yourself! Wow!' Rocky was impressed.

Ben stood next to Fergus, but they weren't talking. Fergus was still staring at the phone in his hand, paying no attention to Ben at all.

Ben didn't know if Fergus was playing a game or texting someone, but he was already beginning to wish he hadn't put up his hand to host a kid from the city.

CHAPTER TWO

Ben stared out the bus window. He could hear the others chattering and joking with their billets behind him.

'What's brown and sticky?' asked Rocky at the top of his voice.

'Yuk!' cried both Angelas at the same time.

'Give up?' asked Rocky.

'What?' said Lim.

'A stick!' Rocky hooted, and everyone groaned and laughed.

Everyone except Ben and Fergus. Fergus didn't even hear the joke, probably, and Ben didn't feel like laughing.

Ben fiddled with a hole in the corner of the seat. Fergus kept right on fiddling with his mobile phone.

'We live out of town,' Ben told him, as the houses grew further and further apart and the footpath disappeared.

But Fergus didn't even look out the window.

The bus rattled over the bridge, past the pine forest and up the hill. At the crest of the hill, the bus stopped and the door opened.

'We get off here,' Ben said. Fergus grabbed his backpack and followed Ben down the steps, still poking at the little device in his hand.

'Watch out you don't get your feet caught in the grid,' warned Ben. 'That's to stop the cattle getting out – they can't walk over it.'

Fergus nodded and jumped over the grid after Ben.

'Our driveway is nearly two kilometres long,' said Ben.

Fergus stopped and looked up the dirt driveway winding over the hill. 'How do we get up there?' he asked in a crisp voice.

'I'll whistle for my horse and we can double-dink up.'

'I'm allergic,' said Fergus.

'Oh,' said Ben. 'Then I guess we walk.'

They plodded up the hill in silence.

Finally Fergus spoke. 'Is there anything to do around here?'

'There's a dead cow in the gully. Do you want to go and look at it?'

'Eww. No,' said Fergus. He looked at his feet and saw that his smart shoes were dusty and dirty. He bent down and wiped them with his hand.

'We could get Dad to take us around the dam on the tractor,' offered Ben.

But Fergus screwed his nose up.

'I've got a tree house. We can play in that? Or we could look for wombats!'

But Fergus wasn't listening. He had gone back to doing whatever it was on his mobile, walking so slowly that he finally stopped altogether on the edge of the driveway.

'Hey,' said Ben, a little crossly.
'I wouldn't stand there if I were you.'

He pointed to the ground at Fergus' feet, where hundreds of huge brown ants were scurrying in and out of a large hole.

'Don't let 'em bite you,' Ben told Fergus. 'It hurts.'

CHAPTER THREE

Fergus froze. An enormous bull ant crawled over his shoe and up onto his sock. Another one followed, then another. Suddenly, Fergus had thrown aside his backpack and was jumping up and down and smacking his legs.

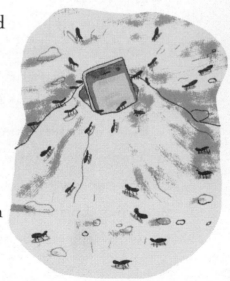

'Aargh!' he screamed. 'I've been bitten!'

His phone fell from his hands, right into

the middle of the ants' nest, caving it in and lodging right inside. In a jiffy there were ants crawling all over it.

'Oh no!' Fergus yelled.

Ben had never seen an ants' nest cave in like that before. But on this day, that's exactly what this one did. And there was no way Ben was putting his hand into it to rescue the phone for Fergus. Ben wasn't sure that he even liked him. He was sick of being ignored. It might be better to leave the stupid phone right where it was. He hated it. Maybe if Fergus didn't have the phone he would talk to Ben and they could do some stuff and have a bit of fun.

But when Ben looked back at Fergus, he saw something that he hadn't expected.

The big boy from the city with the smart shoes and shorts and the sharp haircut and the whiz-bang phone was crying.

Ben didn't know what to do. He wished Mum had come to pick them up instead of them catching the bus. It was supposed to be fun, but it wasn't turning out that way.

Fergus hobbled away from the ants' nest and sat down in the dirt, howling.

'Are you all right?' Ben asked.

But Fergus just blubbered, tears pouring from red eyes, his nose running, and dust and flies sticking to his face.

'Can you walk?' asked Ben.

Fergus shook his head.

What a baby, thought Ben. *It's just a bull ant bite. I've had them before and they're not that bad. Well, if he wants to stay here, he can. I'm going home.*

CHAPTER FOUR

Ben was ready to leave Fergus on the side of the driveway and walk the rest of the way without him. But as he turned and looked at the other boy again, he saw that his eyes had gone all funny and his lips seemed to have blown up like rubber balloons. He was making a terrible noise like a donkey as he tried to breathe and he was holding his chest with both hands. Ben realised Fergus wasn't being a baby. He was in trouble.

Then it hit him. Fergus was allergic to horses; he must be allergic to bull ants, too.

Ben knew he had to act quickly. He had to get Mum down here straight away. He needed that phone. He looked around and found a broken branch from the big gum tree on the hillside. He stripped the leaves off it and then, from a safe distance, poked at the ants' nest to try to ease out the phone. But the dry dirt collapsed more and the phone lodged deeper inside. Bull ants swarmed and ran up the branch towards

Ben. He flicked them off, but they kept coming until finally he had to drop the stick.

Ben shot another look at Fergus. His whole face had blown up and was now red and blotchy. The donkey-breathing noise was getting worse. Fergus had a hand around his throat as though trying to rip it open.

Ben had to get that phone! He ran towards the nest, bent down and plunged his hand in, ignoring the bull ants that ran up his arm and under his shirt. He yanked the mobile out, frantically blew the dirt off it and tapped at it.

Nothing happened.

Ben felt a stinging pain on his neck. Then on his back, and again on his stomach and his arm. He was being bitten all over!

'Come on!' he screamed at the phone, and tapped it again, harder. This time the screen lit up: Enter Passcode. Ben realised straight away that the phone was locked.

'Fergus, what's your PIN?' he yelled. 'Quickly!'

But Fergus' face had turned blue and he could no longer breathe or speak.

How could Ben ring Mum for help if he couldn't unlock the phone? He wished for the first time in his life that he had a mobile of his own. He stared at the screen, close to tears.

Then he noticed two words in tiny print in the bottom corner.

'Emergency Call!'

He punched the screen again, jabbing, jabbing, jabbing.

'Help! Two Gully Farm,' he managed to say, as the pain of more than thirty bull ant bites overcame him and the world went black.

CHAPTER FIVE

Ben felt a cool hand stroking his forehead.

He opened his eyes and sat up. It was Mum. He was in bed, in hospital, wearing only a white gown tied up at the back. There was a tube coming out of his arm, hooked up to a machine with an upside-down bottle of clear liquid.

And there, sitting up in the next bed, with a tube and a machine of his own, looking a little pale but breathing normally and poking at a mobile phone, was the boy from the city.

'Did you know that bull ants are venomous and bite multiple times?' Fergus asked.

'Yeah . . . I worked that out all by myself,' said Ben, feeling the hot, itchy lumps all over his body.

'Bull ant nests sometimes grow to several metres below ground,' Fergus read from the screen on his phone. He looked at Ben. 'Lucky your bull ants didn't have a nest that big,' he said, 'or you'd have fallen in up to your neck and never got my mobile out. Lucky you worked out how to use Emergency Call when the phone was locked. The doctor said you saved my life.'

Wow, Ben thought to himself. *I saved his life. That's massive.* But he also knew he'd nearly left Fergus there. What a close call! He'd never be so quick to accuse anyone of being a baby again.

'Well, I don't know what the other kids have been doing, but I bet none of them have been in an ambulance today,' said Ben's mum brightly. 'Fergus, your mum's coming up from Sydney to take you home, but you will have to come back and visit us again. I know Ben wants to show you his tree house and we'll have a barbecue down by the dam and you can have a tractor ride and . . .'

But both boys were sound asleep, Ben with a little smile on his face, and Fergus with the mobile phone still in his hand.

'Ben, we'll have to get you a mobile phone for Christmas,' she whispered.

THE HOUSE OF PIGGINS

BY R. A. SPRATT

Nanny Piggins, Boris and the children were feeling very sorry for themselves. None of them had sustained an injury. But the most important person in their entire world had. Hans the baker was out of action.

It all started when Nanny Piggins had woken up the previous day with a yen for angel cake. She had immediately kept the children out of school, and gone down to place an order with Hans. He had initially said there was no way he could possibly make 500 angel cakes in just one day, but after Nanny Piggins had shaken him by the collar and beseechingly explained just how much she really needed angel cake, Hans agreed to try his best.

Unfortunately, somewhere around the seventh hour of hand-whipping egg whites (his electric mixer had burnt out after two hours), Hans was stricken with a debilitating pain in his right forearm. And when Nanny Piggins rushed him to the doctor, it was concluded that Hans had baker's elbow – a stress fracture in his ulna – caused by too much whipping.

'What are we going to do?' wailed Nanny Piggins when they returned home after dropping Hans at his flat over the bakery.

'Buy Hans a nice card and perhaps some flowers,' suggested Samantha.

'Yes, of course we'll do that,' said Nanny Piggins. 'But I meant what are we going to do for cake – I'm starving!'

'You could make a cake yourself,' said Derrick.

'No, no, no, that will not do,' said Nanny Piggins. 'I need cake now! If I tried to make cake myself I would just be overcome with hunger and eat all the mixture before I put it in the oven.'

'We could drive into town and find another cake shop,' suggested Samantha.

'No,' sighed Nanny Piggins. 'Their cakes wouldn't be as good as Hans'. It would only remind me of how much I miss him.'

'He's only been out of action for an hour and a half,' said Michael.

Nanny Piggins began to sob. 'Has it been that long already? What am I going to do? Will I ever eat cake again?!'

'I know!' said Derrick. 'Let's drive over to the cake factory in Slimbridge.'

'But it's closed on Saturdays,' said Nanny Piggins.

'We could break in,' suggested Michael.

'No, they've installed new heat-sensing technology and retina eye scanners on all the doors, ever since the last time I let myself in for a little snack,' sighed Nanny Piggins.

'But if we're never going to eat cake again,' said Boris, his lower lip beginning to tremble, 'what are we going to do on my birthday?!' He burst into loud wailing sobs and collapsed on Samantha's shoulder (causing her to collapse and pinning her to the floor).

'There must be somewhere we can go where there's cake,' said Michael. Nanny Piggins instantly snapped out of her

depression and leapt up from the table.
'You're a genius!!!' she exclaimed.

'I am?' asked Michael.

'Oh yes,' said Nanny Piggins, a big smile
on her face. 'Where is the very finest cake
always served on a Saturday afternoon?'

The children looked at each other in
confusion. They had no idea. And Boris was
still weeping too hard to contribute to the
conversation.

'At weddings!' declared Nanny Piggins.
'People are always getting married on
Saturdays and where there is a wedding
there has to be a cake! Usually a great big
delicious cake with lots of marzipan icing
and sugar decorations!'

'But we haven't been invited to any
weddings,' said Samantha.

Nanny Piggins looked down at her
(Samantha was still pinned to the floor) and

smiled fondly. 'The only reason we haven't been invited to any weddings is because the brides and grooms have never had the opportunity to meet us. I'm sure if they had we would have been the first people on their list. We're a lot more fun than a bunch of boring old aunts and cousins.'

'But isn't wedding crashing wrong?' said Derrick.

'It's only wrong if you just eat the cake and leave,' said Nanny Piggins. 'I'm fully prepared to dance with everyone and tell them some of my very best stories. Trust me, by the time we leave they will be pressing extra cake into our pockets.'

——

And so Nanny Piggins, Boris and the children got into Mr Green's car. (They had to throw Mr Green out to do so, because it was Saturday so naturally Mr Green was trying to drive to work. But Nanny Piggins told Mr Green he had to walk because his doctor had rung up saying 'his legs would wither away if he didn't use them at least once a fortnight'.) Then they got Boris to stop crying long enough to get into the car, by reminding him that his birthday was eleven months away and chances were that Hans' stress fracture would be healed by then.

After the initial excitement of heading off to eat cake at a wedding, it soon occurred to them that they had no idea when or where any weddings were occurring.

'Couldn't you use your extraordinary sense of smell to find one?' asked Samantha.

Nanny Piggins leaned out the window and sniffed the air. 'You would think so, but unfortunately the types of distinctively weddingy smells I could normally smell – the fear of the groom, the cooking sherry being secretly drunk by the vicar, or the gaffer tape holding the bride's strapless dress up – are all masked by the mass of flowers in the bouquets and arrangements.'

'Couldn't you sniff for the flowers then?' asked Derrick.

'I could,' agreed Nanny Piggins, 'but flowers are actually quite common in flowerbeds as well. So we could find ourselves drawn into several wild goose chases. So I think the best tactic is to drive around looking for churches surrounded by deliriously happy people throwing rice.'

'Are we going to eat the rice too?' asked Michael.

'No,' said Nanny Piggins. 'For some reason they only throw uncooked rice at weddings. Although, if you think about it, it would make sense to throw cooked rice, preferably something delicious like Thai special fried rice or a nice creamy rice pudding. That way the bride and groom would have something to nibble while they were getting their photos taken.'

'There's one!' screamed Boris.

'One what?!' asked Nanny Piggins, slamming on the brakes of the car. 'A dodo? If so, well spotted because I've always wanted to see one.'

'No, better than that!' said Boris. 'A wedding!'

Sure enough, up ahead was a church with guests pouring out to congratulate a very happy-looking bride and groom.

'Excellent!' exclaimed Nanny Piggins, getting out of the car. 'Come along, children, we must give our best wishes to the lovely couple.'

'Why?' asked Derrick.

'If we just turn up at the wedding and start scoffing cake, that will look suspicious,' said Nanny Piggins. 'We must first establish our cover as invited guests.' With that Nanny Piggins marched across the road, her arms spread wide, calling out, 'My dears, you look breathtaking! I can't wait to get to your reception to celebrate this happy union. Oh, and speaking of which, perhaps you could give me directions to the venue.'

As usual Nanny Piggins was right. They did have a wonderful time at the wedding. Nanny Piggins delighted the other guests with her death-defying stories. She even acted them out (fortunately there was a chandelier for her to swing on and a pair of replica seventeenth-century duelling swords on the wall she could fence with). Then, after the meal, she danced. And, oh, what a dance! Suffice to say, the bride is lucky she married the groom earlier in the day, for if she had not, his head would have been quite turned by Nanny Piggins.

Finally, the moment they had all been waiting for arrived – the cutting of the cake. Nanny Piggins insisted they use a seventeenth-century duelling sword, so they could cut really big pieces. And as soon as she, Boris and the children sank their teeth into their first bite, they knew it had all been worth it. There is something about weddings that brings out the best in people. It is the one day in their life when they say – 'Go on,

put another stick of butter in that cake mix'
and 'Why stop at one? Let's have two inches
of creamy thick icing.'

As a result, the cake was so good that
after one bite you had to quickly take a
drink, because there was so much sugar in
the icing, the process of osmosis caused it
to suck all the moisture out of your mouth.
Nanny Piggins was in heaven. She stopped
speaking altogether for a full two minutes
and just made noises like, 'Mmmm- mm-
mmmm' and 'Aaaaah-mmm' as she ate.

When they finally left the reception after
saying goodbye to everyone and promising
to come to the first anniversary party the
following year, Nanny Piggins, Boris and the
children returned home very satisfied.

'What a wonderful day,' declared Nanny
Piggins.

'It was good cake,' agreed Derrick.

'*Good* is not the word,' exclaimed Nanny Piggins. 'It was *divine*. We'll definitely have to do that again tomorrow.'

'Tomorrow?!' exclaimed Samantha.

'Oh yes,' said Nanny Piggins. 'The doctor said Hans will be out of action for at least a fortnight. I can't go a whole two weeks without eating another cake like that.'

'But Nanny Piggins,' said Samantha. 'It's one thing to gatecrash *one* wedding. But to gatecrash *two* weddings. That's just naughty.'

'Don't worry,' said Nanny Piggins. 'I wasn't planning to gatecrash two weddings.'

'Good,' sighed Samantha.

'I was planning to gatecrash another three,' said Nanny Piggins, taking out a crumpled list from her pocket. 'The caterer gave me the skinny on where all the weddings are happening across town tomorrow.'

'We're going to gatecrash three weddings in one day?' asked Derrick.

'Don't think of it as gatecrashing,' advised Nanny Piggins. 'Gatecrashing is wrong. No, what we are doing is providing entertainment in the form of our delightful company in exchange for a small sample of their wedding cake.'

'Today you ate the entire second tier of the wedding cake all on your own,' reminded Samantha.

'For which the bride should thank me,' said Nanny Piggins. 'You know what humans are like. Always watching their weight. She should be grateful I saved her from having all that cake lying around her home tempting her.'

And so, the next morning, Nanny Piggins, Boris and the children put on their best party clothes and headed out to celebrate the institution of marriage, again. Despite the children's concerns about being thrown in jail for the serial theft of cake, they ended up having a wonderful day.

All the weddings were very different. The Wong–Yap wedding had lion dancers (although Nanny Piggins could not understand why they used men in lion suits and not real lions). The Fitzgerald–FitzSimons wedding had a bouncy castle, which was a good idea in theory, but not so good in practice at an event where people are eating large amounts of food. (Fortunately the maître d' had a hose handy.) But the Lee–Edwards wedding was the best as far as Nanny Piggins was concerned because they had a chocolate fountain. You were meant to dip strawberries in it. But no one noticed when Nanny Piggins stuck her whole head under the warm chocolately flow (although it did have a spectacular effect on her hairstyle, and her hat was lost for three hours, until the father of the bride dipped in a strawberry and drew out the elegant bonnet).

Nanny Piggins, Boris and the children returned home that night, very tired and very full of cake.

'Well, that was fun,' admitted Samantha, 'but we aren't going wedding crashing tomorrow, are we? We have school. And no one gets married on a Monday.'

'No, there will be no more wedding crashing,' agreed Nanny Piggins.

The children were relieved. After four weddings in two days they felt if they ate any more they would explode.

'The wedding cakes were good, delicious even,' continued Nanny Piggins. 'But there was something lacking. I thought there was room for improvement.'

'But you cried when you ate the chocolate orange layer cake at the Wong–Yap wedding because it tasted so good,' said Michael.

'Yes, but I was very hungry at the time,' said Nanny Piggins. 'It was only when I ate my eighth slice that I began to realise there was room for improvement. Where were the chocolate chunks? Where were the chocolate sprinkles?'

The children had no answers for these rhetorical questions.

'Why were none of the four wedding cakes entirely dipped in chocolate?' asked Nanny Piggins.

The children did not know.

'It certainly would have been easy enough at the Lee–Edwards wedding. The chocolate fountain was right there,' added Boris.

'The world of wedding cake creation is obviously crying out for a new creative influence, a baker with a genius for cake, icing and visionary design,' said Nanny Piggins. 'In short – they need me.'

'What are you planning to do?' asked Samantha, beginning to suspect that perhaps she would not be going to school tomorrow after all.

'I am going to open "The House of Piggins",' said Nanny Piggins.

'Why is she opening a house?' asked Michael.

'I think Nanny Piggins is talking about starting a wedding-cake-baking business,' explained Derrick.

'Piffle to that!' admonished Nanny Piggins. 'The House of Piggins will be more than a cake-baking business. It will be a design studio for cake-based art.'

———

And so The House of Piggins went into business and it was immediately a huge success. If anything, it was too successful, because the cakes were so good. If guests knew a House of Piggins cake was going to be served, they started yelling 'Get on with it' and 'Where's the cake?' in the middle of the marriage ceremony.

At one wedding the bride actually bolted halfway through the vows, not because she wanted to run out on the groom (she married him at a second ceremony later in the day) but because she wanted to get to the reception before anybody else and start eating the cake. (She had bought a wedding dress with an elasticised waist especially so she could eat lots and lots of it.)

The vicar was very cross with Nanny Piggins. 'Everyone has gathered here to celebrate the sanctity of marriage and that has been ruined by your cake,' he accused.

'Pish!' retorted Nanny Piggins. 'My cakes are single-handedly propping up the marriage rate. You should be thanking me. I'm bringing you business.'

'But the institution of marriage is the most important thing about a wedding day,' argued the vicar.

'And it would be a much happier institution if married people ate more cake,' argued Nanny Piggins.

'I refuse to conduct any more weddings where you supply the cake,' shouted the vicar.

'I refuse to supply my cake to any more of your ceremonies!' countered Nanny Piggins. She turned on her heel and marched out of the church. The children hurried after her.

'But Nanny Piggins,' said Michael, 'you love making wedding cakes.'

'Oh, I'm not quitting the wedding-cake business,' declared Nanny Piggins. 'I'm diversifying. I'm going to become a wedding celebrant! From now on I will supply the cake and the marriage ceremony.'

And she was true to her word, which meant the vicar soon found himself with a lot more free Saturdays because 'The House of Piggins Wedding Ceremonies' became an instant hit.

Nanny Piggins solved the problem of having guests and bridal party members making an undignified dash for the cake by borrowing her old cannon from the circus and starting each of her ceremonies by blasting cake over the congregation. She spattered them with delicious chocolate cake, lemon drizzle cake or sticky toffee surprise cake – whatever the bride and groom requested. The congregation enjoyed eating the impromptu snacks they scraped off their clothes, and it was quite an ice-breaker. (It also made Nanny Piggins tremendously popular with all the local drycleaners.)

The House of Piggins Wedding Ceremonies was doing a roaring trade.

Nanny Piggins, Boris and the children spent all week making the most fantastic cakes her mind could imagine (and she had quite an imagination when it came to cake) and then they would spend all Saturday and Sunday running one wedding after another.

———

One Monday morning after a particularly exhausting weekend of cake, cake and more cake, Nanny Piggins, Boris and the children were sitting around the kitchen table, girding themselves for another long week of cake-baking ahead (by eating a slice of cake) when they were interrupted by a knock at the door.

'I wonder who that could be?' said Boris.

'If it is a young couple wanting to get married,' said Nanny Piggins, 'tell them I've got a three-year waiting list for a full marriage service. Or they can come in now and I'll marry them while I start work on the next cake, then to celebrate I'll let them lick the spoon.'

Michael rushed back a moment later. 'It's not a couple,' he said. 'It's a Herald.'

'As in "Hark the Herald Angels Sing"?' asked Nanny Piggins.

A man dressed in purple tights, crimson bloomers and an old-fashioned velvet tunic with gold trim stepped into the room, and blew a trill on a trumpet. Everyone flinched, partly because unaccompanied trumpet music is dreadful, but mainly because it is a tremendously loud noise in an enclosed space.

'Hark,' said the Herald.

'Ooo, it is just like in the song,' said Nanny Piggins.

'I come with great tidings from the Royal Palace of Molavadina,' said the

Herald. 'Her Royal Highness the Princess Annabelle has requested your immediate presence in the principality, to assist in the preparations for her imminent nuptials.'

'Her immi-what-whats?' asked Nanny Piggins.

'She's getting married soon,' explained Samantha.

'Ooooh,' said Nanny Piggins, catching on. 'The Princess wants a cake.'

'His Royal Highness the King of Molavadina,' continued the Herald, 'has a private jet waiting to fly you out to the principality immediately.'

'I will need to bring my elite cake-making team,' said Nanny Piggins shrewdly.

'Who?' asked Michael.

'Shhh,' chided Derrick. 'I think she means us.'

'Of course,' said the Herald. 'His Highness has decreed that no expense be spared in making Princess Annabelle the finest wedding cake ever made.'

'That would have to be pretty fine,' said Nanny Piggins. 'I made a triple-choc fudge cake last week that was dangerously good.'

The children nodded their agreement. (In the end Nanny Piggins had decided the cake was too good to use at a wedding and they had eaten it all themselves. Nanny Piggins reasoned that it would be unfair to start the young couple off with a cake that good, because then they would spend every day for the rest of their marriage moaning about how they wanted another slice.)

———

Nanny Piggins and her elite cake-making team soon arrived at Molavadina. (She had recruited Hans into the team because she thought she could use some professional help. And also because she still felt guilty about his accident, and wanted him to have a nice overseas holiday.) The capital was a beautiful city with cobbled roads, and narrow little shops weaving up the steep hillside to the royal castle at the cliff top overlooking the sea. When they got to the castle they were immediately taken to meet Princess Annabelle.

Nanny Piggins instantly knew she was in the presence of a kindred spirit, for the Princess was eerily beautiful, which was surprising because extremely chubby women are not normally thought of as the beautiful type. But Annabelle was undeniably so, particularly when she spoke of cake. The happy subject made her cheeks glow and her eyes sparkle.

'Now,' said Nanny Piggins, 'I am planning to make you my standard wedding cake. That is an octo-choc-chocolate cake with extra chocolate.'

'What's that?' asked Princess Annabelle.

'A chocolate cake with chocolate icing, chocolate filling, chocolate sprinkles, chocolate chips, solid chocolate base, solid chocolate on top, and chocolate cream,' explained Nanny Piggins. 'Have I forgotten a chocolate?'

'Entirely dipped in chocolate,' reminded Michael, who had been counting them off on his fingers.

'Oh yes,' said Nanny Piggins.

'That's eight types of chocolate,' said the Princess. 'But what about the *extra* chocolate?'

'It is served with a piece of chocolate on the side,' explained Nanny Piggins.

'That sounds perfect,' exclaimed the Princess, clapping her hands with delight. 'Do you have a picture you could show me?'

'Of course,' said Nanny Piggins, handing Princess Annabelle a sheet of paper. 'Here is a drawing I whipped up on the plane.'

'Oh,' said the Princess, her face dropping slightly. 'It looks delicious, but it just looks like a regular chocolate wedding cake.'

Nanny Piggins smiled. 'That is because it is a scale drawing. You see the bride and groom on the top of the cake?' Nanny Piggins pointed to the figurines at the top of her design.

'The little figurines, yes,' said the Princess.

'They aren't little figurines,' explained Nanny Piggins. 'That's you and the Duke. I am making a cake big enough to have real people as the cake toppers.'

Princess Annabelle's eyes boggled. 'But then the cake must be ten metres tall!'

'Fifteen,' corrected Nanny Piggins. 'I don't believe in half measures.'

'I love it!' cried the Princess. 'I must have this cake.'

'But that's not all,' said Nanny Piggins. 'I've spoken to some of my friends at NASA, and in exchange for my ongoing silence about a certain international incident that took place earlier in the year, they are lending me a hydraulic system.'

'I don't understand,' said the Princess.

'After the ceremony,' explained Nanny Piggins, 'you will be lowered by hydraulics into the cake, so you and your groom can eat your way out while the guests eat their way in.'

Princess Annabelle started to cry tears of joy. She also hugged Nanny Piggins tightly while sobbing, 'Thank you, thank you all of you. This is going to be the best wedding ever.'

————

So Nanny Piggins and her team set to work. It was a good job they brought Hans with them. His piping skills were invaluable and by sitting up on Boris' head, he was able to reach up to decorate the first three metres of the cake. (He had recovered well from his baker's elbow.) Plus it turned out that Hans knew quite a lot about cake engineering. It was his idea to insert long chocolate rods into the cake for extra support.

When the big day arrived, the cake-makers were exhausted but proud. Not since the construction of the Taj Mahal had a man-made (or in this case pig-made) structure been assembled that was so magnificent. Tourists were already coming to the island just to have their picture taken with it (and secretly lick the icing when no one was looking).

The wedding was to be held at midday, so after she finished piping the entire first chapter of her favourite romance novel along the side of the cake, Nanny Piggins got dressed in her marriage celebrant's robes (an off-the-shoulder evening dress made entirely out of chocolate bar wrappers, which still contained chocolate, just in case she got peckish during the ceremony) and went down to the castle courtyard where the wedding was to be held.

As Nanny Piggins stood on top of the giant cake facing the Duke of Sloblavia (having been raised up there in a cherry picker), she got her first good look at the groom. He was tall, which Nanny Piggins knew from reading romance novels was supposed to count for something. And his face was classically handsome. But he was not an attractive man because the expression on his face was so miserable.

'Have you recently lost a pet?' Nanny Piggins enquired sympathetically.

'I'm not here to make chit-chat. Why can't we just get on with it?' asked the Duke stroppily.

'Because the bride hasn't arrived yet,' explained Nanny Piggins slowly, beginning to be concerned the poor groom had suffered a head injury.

'That would be right . . .' muttered the groom. 'Typical woman.'

'What did you say?' asked Nanny Piggins, beginning to glower.

But at this moment they were interrupted by Michael rushing to the side of the cake and yelling up, 'Nanny Piggins, you'd better come quickly!'

'What's the matter?' called down Nanny Piggins.

'Probably can't decide which shoes to wear,' muttered the groom. 'Ridiculous females.'

Nanny Piggins turned back to bite him, but Michael wailed, 'Please, Nanny Piggins, come quickly.' She slid down the solid chocolate fireman's pole conveniently built into the back of the cake (all structures over ten metres' tall have to have an emergency exit) and hurried off with Michael.

————

When Nanny Piggins arrived at the Princess' bedroom it was to find Her Royal Highness face down on her bed, weeping loudly.

'What's the matter?' asked Nanny Piggins. 'She hasn't lost a pet, has she? I don't understand why everyone is in such a bad mood. In most countries weddings are celebrated as happy occasions.'

'Tell Nanny Piggins what you told us,' Samantha urged.

Princess Annabelle raised her face from her pillow long enough to wail, 'I don't want to marry the Duke!' before breaking into wracking sobs.

'Then why on earth did you say you would?' asked Nanny Piggins.

'I just wanted a wedding so I could have one of your wedding cakes,' sobbed the Princess.

'Oooooh,' said Nanny Piggins. As a cake lover herself, this made complete sense to her. 'But you didn't need to get engaged to that awful man just to have one of my cakes,' said Nanny Piggins, sitting down next to the Princess and giving her a hug.

'But Daddy wouldn't have paid for it unless it was for a wedding,' said the Princess.

'Nanny Piggins would have made you a cake anyway,' said Derrick. 'She makes cakes for everyone.'

'When you have a talent such as mine it is important to share it,' agreed Nanny Piggins.

'But you needed Daddy's deposit to rent the hydraulic system from NASA,' wept the Princess. 'I thought a lifetime of being married to a miserable bore would be worth it for the chance of being lowered into a fifteen-metre-high octo-choc-chocolate cake with extra chocolate, and eating my way out. But now I realise it's not.'

'Tell Nanny Piggins the rest,' urged Samantha.

'There's more?!' asked Nanny Piggins, thinking this day was getting to be even more exciting and dramatic than an episode of *The Young and the Irritable*.

'I've fallen in love with another,' sobbed Princess Annabelle.

'With another wedding cake?' asked Nanny Piggins. She was struggling to keep up.

'Oh no,' Princess Annabelle assured her, clutching Nanny Piggins' hand. 'My heart is forever true to your cake. No, I've fallen in love with another man.'

'Really?' said Nanny Piggins, thinking of all the very unimpressive courtiers she had met during her stay and trying to work out which one was the least revolting. 'Who?'

Princess Annabelle began to look a little sheepish at this point. 'Hans,' she whispered.

'The baker?!' yelped Nanny Piggins. She did not begrudge Hans the happiness of having a Royal Princess fall in love with him – no one deserved joy more than him after all the cake-related bliss he brought to others. But the thought of anyone loving Hans entirely took her by surprise. You see, Nanny Piggins was so in love with Hans' baked goods, it never occurred to her to think of him in any other way.

'These past few days, watching him beat eggs, melt butter and wedge silver balls into four-inch thick chocolate icing – he stole my heart. I've never seen a more attractive man,' gushed Princess Annabelle.

'Of course,' said Nanny Piggins. Now that she thought about it she realised that falling in love with a master baker was the most sensible thing she had ever heard of. It was a wonder that there weren't hordes of women in love with Hans and trying to beat down his shop door. But most people are terribly superficial and would be put off by the fact that he was very short and hairy. (If he was not a man, Hans would have made an excellent bearded lady.)

'But now Daddy is going to make me marry that odious Duke,' wept Princess Annabelle.

'He smells as well?' asked Nanny Piggins. 'Who knew one man could have so very many faults.'

'We can't let Princess Annabelle marry into a lifetime of misery,' said Samantha.

'Of course not,' agreed Nanny Piggins. 'If I did, I'd have to hand in my *The Young and the Irritable* fan club card from shame.'

'But what can we do?' asked Derrick. 'This is a castle surrounded by guards, and built on an island in the middle of the sea. They aren't going to let us just waltz off with their Princess.'

Nanny Piggins was rubbing her snout – something she always did when she was thinking hard. 'Don't worry, I am having the beginnings of a brilliant idea,' said Nanny Piggins.

———

A short time later, Nanny Piggins was standing toe to toe with Princess Annabelle's father, yelling at him.

'If you can't find the Princess, then I'm taking my cake and going home!' yelled Nanny Piggins.

'The wedding will go ahead as planned and that is an order!' barked the King.

'Your men have been searching for an hour and they haven't found the Princess or the baker she fell in love with. I can't dillydally here all day, I've got the Partridge–Dingleberry wedding cake to make back at home,' said Nanny Piggins.

'Fine,' said the King. 'Take your cake and go! I've got better things to do than stand around arguing with a pig.'

'I didn't know you were arguing with the Duke as well,' said Nanny Piggins, looking over her shoulder to see if he was there.

'He means you,' said Derrick.

'He does? Oh yes, of course, even I forget I'm a pig sometimes,' said Nanny Piggins.

The King was just leaving the room to find some more people to yell at when Nanny Piggins called after him. 'May we borrow your biggest helicopter? It's just that

I don't think the airlines will let us take on a fifteen-metre-tall cake as hand luggage.'

'Do what you like,' snapped the King.

Ten minutes later Nanny Piggins, Boris and the children were safely inside the helicopter and flying back home. And as I'm sure you have cleverly figured out, Princess Annabelle and Hans the baker were hidden inside the cake, which was hanging beneath the helicopter as it sped over the ocean.

'Do you think they're all right down there in the cake?' asked Samantha.

'Of course they are,' said Nanny Piggins. 'They have each other, they have true love, and they have three metric tonnes of octo-choc-chocolate cake. What more could a young couple ask for?'

FITNESS FANATICS

BY SALLY GOULD

FITNESS FANATICS

Zack stood on the freshly mown oval. It was empty. The other kids weren't allowed on it until Fitness Fanatics finished. He listened to Mr Bannister giving his usual speech.

'You've got to run past the red flag before it's counted as a lap. Some kids don't seem to know how to count,' he boomed. Everyone laughed. 'I don't want anyone to drop dead. But I'd like to see my Fitness Fanatics push themselves.'

The kids grinned.

Zack knew that Mr Bannister wanted to make one of his Fitness Fanatics a State Champion runner. Just like he had been.

Mr Bannister looked at Zack. 'Are you chewing gum?'

Zack swallowed and shook his head.

Mr Bannister rolled his eyes and then looked at Smithy. 'Charlie Smith! Get that jumper off!'

Smithy took it off and tied it around his waist. He gave Mr Bannister a mischievous grin.

Mr Bannister then looked Ben up and down. 'You've got school shoes on. What's your name?'

'Ben, sir.'

'Why haven't I seen you before?'

'I'm new, sir.'

'Oh,' Mr Bannister's voice softened. 'Next week bring your runners. And no one calls me "sir". Okay?'

The kids all laughed and yelled out, 'No, sir!'

Mr Bannister tried to look cross, but laughed instead.

Ben blushed.

Zack elbowed Smithy. 'The new boy's tall.' He stood straighter. 'Look at his skinny legs.'

'Yeah.' Smithy put his hands on his hips. 'Look how long they are.' He glanced down at his own short legs. 'He could be fast.'

Zack stuck out his chest. 'Not as fast as us.'

The kids took their positions. Mr Bannister blew his whistle, and Zack and Smithy sprinted out in front until the older kids overtook them. Mr Bannister ran up and down one side of the oval, yelling encouragement. Zack and Smithy did their usual ten laps, then went over to Mr Bannister's Grade Six helper to get ten stickers each for their Fitness Fanatics books.

Mr Bannister joined them. 'Lazy Bones 1 and Lazy Bones 2,' he teased. 'You both could've done two more laps!'

'Don't wanna be tired for PE,' replied Zack. Mr Bannister shook his head, then went off to yell encouragement to the remaining runners.

Ben ran past them.

'He's still going,' said Smithy.

Zack frowned.

'Look at him. Those long legs make it look easy.' Smithy lowered his voice. 'He might win the cross country.'

Zack folded his arms. *Not if I can help it*, he thought.

Ben stopped after thirteen laps. Then he stretched his legs like a professional athlete. They watched him. Then they gave each other a look that said, 'Far out!'

Mr Bannister couldn't stop smiling. He gave Ben a Fitness Fanatics book with thirteen stickers and slapped him on the back. 'Mate, you're a natural.'

Ben blushed.

Zack kicked the grass. *Thirteen laps at Fitness Fanatics doesn't prove anything*, he thought. *I'm the best runner in Grade Three and I'm going to win the cross country.*

THE HOLE

Zack, Smithy and Ben stood in the shade of the old gum tree the next week at Fitness Fanatics. Zack blew a bubble with his gum. 'I'm doing thirteen laps today,' he said.

Smithy put his hands on his hips. 'Ten's enough for me.'

'When's the cross country?' asked Ben.

'Next month,' said Smithy. 'This year we run through the Wetlands Reserve.' He took off his jumper and tied it around his waist.

'Yeah,' added Zack, 'most of the kids end up walking it. You have to be fit.'

They took their positions alongside the other kids. Mr Bannister blew the whistle. Ben got a good start. Zack and Smithy slipped behind. Zack could see Ben keeping up with the Grade Four kids. He took long strides with his long legs. *He's a good runner*, Zack admitted as he pushed himself harder. He'd need to train more to beat Ben.

A small white dog with honey-coloured markings joined Zack and Smithy as they ran.

'Honey,' shouted Zack, 'where've ya been?' Honey barked and ran alongside him.

His legs felt heavier as he watched Ben increase his lead. Then Zack couldn't believe his eyes. Ben fell flat on his face.

'Far out!' Smithy cried. By the time they reached the place where Ben had fallen, he'd limped off the oval.

Zack saw the hole; it was small and deep. After ten laps he stopped. What was the point? He'd already beaten Ben.

Smithy only managed eight laps. He clutched his stomach. 'I shouldn't have eaten that meat pie.'

They headed towards Ben, who was resting on a bench. Zack whispered to Smithy, 'If he was such a good runner he'd miss the holes.'

Ben's knee was bandaged.

Zack slapped him on the shoulder. 'Bad luck,' he said.

A PAINFUL FALL

The next week before Fitness Fanatics Ben changed into his runners.

'Is your leg okay?' Zack asked.

'It wasn't that bad.'

That day Zack did eleven laps of the oval. He'd planned to do thirteen, but he was tired. He'd stayed up too late the night before.

Smithy was red in the face when he joined Zack. He looked over at the other runners. 'Far out! Ben's still going.'

Ben finally joined them after he'd done fifteen laps. He was puffing hard.

Next time I'll do sixteen, Zack told himself.

———

Zack sat on top of the monkey bars at recess the next day. 'Look at me,' he yelled out to Smithy and Ben. Then Zack fell back and swung from the back of his knees. He swung back and forth and scratched himself under the arms. 'I'm a monkey,' he called out.

Smithy laughed. 'You're ugly enough.'

Zack poked out his tongue.

'Your face is really red,' said Ben.

'It's a rush; feels real good.' Zack swung back and forth, higher and higher. Then he went too high and his knees lost their grip.

He screamed before falling in a heap and twisting his ankle. The pain was unbearable. *Oh no! Oh no!* he screamed inside his head. *I'll never win the cross country now!*

TRAINING

Zack watched the Fitness Fanatics the next week. Ben came along and sat down on the bench next to him. He looked down at Zack's bandaged ankle. 'How is it?'

'Okay,' replied Zack. 'Aren't you running?'

'I don't feel like it.' They watched Smithy, wearing his jumper, take off with the other kids. Honey appeared and grabbed Mr Bannister's red flag with her mouth. She tore off with it. Zack and Ben laughed as they watched the Grade Six helper run after her.

'When your ankle gets better . . . do you want to train together?' asked Ben.

Zack squinted. 'You and me? Together?' *Far out*, he thought. *I wanna beat him, not train with him.*

'We could practise the cross-country route,' Ben said excitedly. 'Smithy, too.'

I'd get faster, thought Zack. *And if Ben trains and I don't . . . he'll thrash me.* Zack nodded. 'Okay.'

———

When Zack's ankle was better, he asked his mum if he could run with Ben at the Wetlands Reserve. She said no. He followed her out to the back verandah and asked again.

'No,' she said. 'You can practise on the school oval.' She turned back to her painting.

He punched the wooden rail. 'It's not the same!' he yelled. 'Ben's allowed to go.'

'Well you're not,' she said as she made the sea wild with strokes of her paintbrush. 'And if you ask again, I won't let you go to the oval!'

Zack stormed to his bedroom.

———

After school every day for the next three weeks, Zack met Ben on the oval. They trained for a whole hour. Smithy didn't want to train every day. He had told them he was going to be a pilot when he grew up, not a runner.

On the first day, Zack could barely keep up with Ben. Not that he'd admit it. After sixteen laps, he puffed and panted and thought he was about to drop dead. But he felt better when Ben fell on the ground complaining that his legs had turned to mush.

After two weeks Zack and Ben were doing twenty laps of the oval. After three weeks they were doing twenty laps without feeling like they were about to die. Zack no longer went too fast at the beginning. And now he breathed evenly the whole time.

On the last day at the end of training they stretched their legs. Zack said, 'All this training better be worth it.'

'It will,' replied Ben.

'Thanks,' said Zack as he held his ankle.

'What for?'

Zack jumped up. 'Race you to the front gate.'

Ben jumped up and raced after him.

THE CROSS COUNTRY

Mr Bannister paced up and down in front of the Grade Three kids. They wore their house colours of red, blue, green or yellow.

Zack and Ben looked at each other and grinned.

Smithy stood next to them. 'May the best man win,' he said.

'Is everyone ready?' yelled Mr Bannister.

'Yes!' screamed the kids.

Mr Bannister looked at Zack. 'No gum today?'

'No, sir.'

'Smithy, no jumper!' Mr Bannister grinned. 'Excellent. Now remember, everybody, follow the red arrows and you'll be on the right track.' He blew the whistle and, in a sea of colour, the kids took off on the track alongside the bush.

Within five minutes, Zack, Ben and Smithy were out in front. Zack felt fantastic. He could do this every day. Maybe he'd train for the Olympics. He imagined running around a track in a stadium full of cheering people.

Five minutes later, Smithy slowed down. 'You guys keep going,' he panted. 'Third place is good enough for me.'

Zack and Ben surged ahead, following the red arrows. They reached the lake where there were hundreds of birds. Zack was sure they'd break a record. Did the school keep records? Yeah, Mr Bannister was obsessed. He'd keep records.

They left the lake and reached a rickety bridge that crossed a shallow gully. But the track divided into two and there was no red arrow! Zack and Ben suddenly stopped.

'Which way?' panted Zack.

Ben looked worried. Zack had never seen him look worried. 'We'll just have to run until we see the next red arrow,' said Ben. He looked at the bridge and turned to Zack. 'Over or under?'

'Over.'

They ran for several minutes without seeing a red arrow. Zack was about to suggest they turn back when he saw a dog with a mouthful of red arrows.

'Honey!' he yelled. 'Where did you get the arrows?'

Honey looked pleased with herself. She scooted off back to the bridge, the arrows still in her mouth.

Zack and Ben looked at each other and took off in the same direction. Zack had

never run so fast in his life. When they got to the bridge, a teacher told the kids which track to take. They were way behind now.

Zack didn't think they could run any faster but they did. They overtook about twenty kids before they reached the oval. They could see Smithy half a lap away from the finish line. They'd never catch him. But they could come second.

Somehow they sped up. Every part of Zack's body ached. They overtook the last two kids who were behind Smithy. Zack saw him cross the finish line. Zack and Ben were neck and neck. Zack could hear Mr Bannister and Smithy cheering them on. As they crossed the line they raised their hands and slapped them together.

They hadn't won, but they were the best runners. And the best of friends!

SOUPERMAN

BY PAUL JENNINGS

'Look at this school report,' said Dad. 'It's a disgrace. Four D's and two E's. It's the worst report I have ever seen.'

He was starting to go red in the face. I knew I was in big trouble. I had to do something. And fast.

'I did my best,' I said feebly.

'Nonsense,' he yelled. 'Look what it says down the bottom here. Listen to this.'

Robert could do much better. He has not done enough work this term. He spends all his time at school reading Superman comics under the desk.

'That's it,' he raved on. 'That's the end of all this Superman silliness. You can get all those Superman comics, all those posters and all the rest of your Superman junk and take it down to the council rubbish bin now.'

'But, Dad,' I gasped.

'No buts, I said now and I mean now.' His voice was getting louder and louder. I decided to do what he wanted before he freaked out altogether. I walked slowly into the bedroom and picked up every one of my sixty Superman comics. Then I trudged out of the door and into the corridor. We lived on the first floor of the high-rise flats so I took the lift down to the council rubbish bin. It was one of those big steel bins that can only be lifted up by a special garbage truck. I could only just reach the top of it by standing on tiptoes. I shoved the comics over the edge and then caught the lift back to the first floor.

That was when I first met Superman.

He was making a tremendous racket
in flat 132b. It sounded as if someone
was rattling the window. It can be very
dangerous banging on the windows when
you live upstairs. At first I thought it was
probably some little kid trying to get outside
while his mother was away shopping.
I decided to do the right thing and go and
save him. I pushed open the door, which
wasn't locked, and found myself in the
strangest room I had ever seen.

The walls of the flat were completely
lined with cans of soup. Thousands
and thousands of cans were stacked on
bookshelves going right up to the ceiling.
It was a bit like a supermarket.

Then I noticed something even stranger.
I looked over at the window and saw
someone trying to get in. I couldn't believe

my eyes. It was him. It was really him.
My hero – Superman. In person.

He was clinging to the outside ledge
and trying to open the window. He was
puffing and blowing and couldn't seem to
lift it up. Every now and then he looked
down as if he was frightened of falling. I ran
over to the window and undid the catch.
I pulled up the window and Superman
jumped in.

———

He looked just as he did in the comics.
He was wearing a red cape and a
blue-and-red outfit with a large 'S' on
his chest. He had black curly hair and a
handsome face. His body rippled with
muscles.

'Thanks,' he said. 'You came just in time.
I couldn't hang on much longer.'

My mouth fell open. 'But what about your power?' I asked him. 'Why didn't you just smash the window open?'

He smiled at me. Then he held one finger over his mouth and went over and closed the door I had left open. 'My power only lasts for half an hour,' he said. 'I had to go all the way to Tasmania to rescue a woman lost in the snow. I only just made it back to the window when my power ran out. That's why I couldn't get the window open.'

'Half an hour?' I said. 'Superman's power doesn't last for half an hour. It lasts forever.'

'You've been reading too many comics,' he responded. 'It's S-o-u-p-e-r-m-a-n, not S-u-p-e-r-m-a-n. I get half an hour of power from each can of soup.'

I started to get nervous. This bloke was a nut. He was dressed up in a Superman outfit and he had the story all wrong. He thought Superman's power came from drinking cans of soup. I started to walk towards the door. I had to get out of there.

'Come back, and I'll show you,' he said. He went over to the fridge and tried to lift it up. He couldn't. He strained until drops of sweat appeared on his forehead but the fridge didn't budge. Next, he picked up one of the cans of soup and tried to squeeze it. Nothing happened. He couldn't get it open.

'See,' he went on. 'I'm as weak as a kitten. That proves that I have no power.'

'But it doesn't prove that you're Superman,' I said.

He walked over to a drawer and took out a bright blue can-opener. Then he took out a book and flipped over the pages. 'Here it is,' he exclaimed. 'Lifting up refrigerators. Pea and ham soup.'

He took down the can of pea and ham soup from the shelf and opened it with the

bright blue can-opener.
The he drank the lot.
Raw. Straight out of
the can.

'Ugh,' I yelled.
'Don't drink it raw.'

'I have to,' he said.
'I don't have time to
heat it up. Just imagine
if I got a call to save
someone who had fallen
from a building. They
would be smashed to bits
on the ground before the soup was warm.'

He walked over to the fridge and lifted
it up with one hand. He actually did it.
He lifted the fridge high above his head
with one hand. I couldn't believe it. The
soup seemed to give him superhuman
strength.

'Fantastic,' I shouted. 'No one except Superman could lift a fridge. Do you really get your power from cans of soup?'

He didn't answer. Instead he did a long, loud burp. Then he held his hand up over his mouth and went red in the face. 'Sorry,' he said. 'I've got a stomach-ache. It always happens after I drink the soup too quickly. I'll just nick into the bathroom and get myself an Alka-Seltzer for this indigestion.'

Indigestion. Superman doesn't get indigestion. He is like the Queen or the Pope. He just doesn't have those sorts of problems and he doesn't burp, either. It wouldn't be right. That's when I knew he was a fake. I decided to try the soup out myself while he was in the bathroom and prove that it was all nonsense.

I looked at the book which had the list of soups. There was a different soup named for every emergency. For burst dams it was beef broth. For stopping trains it was cream of tomato. Celery soup was for rescuing people from floods.

I decided to try the chicken soup. It was for smashing down doors. I picked up the bright blue can-opener and used it on a can of chicken soup I found on the top shelf. I drank the whole lot. Cold and raw. Then I went over to the door and punched it with my fist.

Nothing happened to the door but my poor fingers were skinned to the bone. The pain was awful. My eyes started to water. 'You fake,' I yelled through the bathroom door. 'You rotten fake.' I rushed out of the flat as fast as I could go. I was really mad at that phoney Souperman. He was a big disappointment. I wished I could meet the real Superman. The one in the comics.

My comics! I needed them badly. I wanted
to read about the proper Superman
who didn't eat cans of raw soup and get
indigestion. I wondered if the garbage truck
had taken the comics yet. There might still
be time to get them back. It had taken me
three years to save them all. I didn't care
what Dad said, I was going to keep those
comics. I rushed down to the council bin as
fast as I could.

I couldn't see inside the bin because
it was too high but I knew by the smell
that it hadn't been emptied. I jumped up,
grabbed the edge and pulled myself over
the top. What a stink. It was putrid. The
bin contained broken eggshells, old bones,
hundreds of empty soup cans, a dead cat and
other foul muck. I couldn't see my comics
anywhere, so I started to dig around looking

for them. I was so busy looking for the comics that I didn't hear the garbage truck coming until it was too late.

With a lurch, the bin was lifted into the air and tipped upside down. I was dumped into the back of the garbage truck with all the filthy rubbish. I was buried under piles of plastic bags, bottles and kitchen scraps. I couldn't breathe. I knew that if I didn't get to the top I would suffocate.

After what seemed like hours I managed to dig my way up to the surface. I looked up with relief at the flats towering above and at the clouds racing across the sky. Then something happened that made my heart stop. The rubbish started to move. The driver had started the crusher on the truck and it was pushing all the rubbish up to one end and squashing it. A great steel blade was moving towards me. I was about to be flattened inside a pile of garbage. What a way to die.

'Help,' I screamed. 'Help.' It was no use. The driver couldn't see me. No one could see me. Except Souperman. He was sitting on the window ledge of his room and banging a can of soup on the wall. He was trying to open it.

The great steel blade came closer and closer. My ribs were hurting. A great pile of rubbish was rising around me like a swelling tide and pushing me upwards and squeezing me at the same time. By now I could just see over the edge of the truck. There was no one in sight. I looked up again at Souperman. 'Forget the stupid soup,' I yelled. 'Get me out of here or I will be killed.'

Souperman looked down at me from the first-floor window and shook his head. He looked scared. Then, without warning, and

with the unopened
can of soup still
in his hand, he
jumped out of
the window.

Did he fly
through the air in
the manner of a
bird? No way. He fell
to the ground like a
human brick and thudded onto the footpath
not far from the truck. He lay there in a
crumpled heap.

I tried to scream but I couldn't. The
crusher had pushed all the air out of my
lungs. It was squeezing me tighter and
tighter. I knew I had only seconds to live.

I looked over at Souperman. He was
alive. He was groaning and still trying to
open the can of soup. From somewhere deep

in my lungs I managed to find one more breath. 'Leave the soup,' I gasped, 'and turn off the engine.'

He nodded and started crawling slowly and painfully towards the truck. His face was bleeding and he had a black eye but he kept going. With a soft moan, he pulled himself up to the truck door and opened it.

'Switch off the engine,' I heard him tell the driver. Then everything turned black and I heard no more.

The next thing I remember was lying on the footpath with Souperman and the driver bending over me.

'Don't worry,' said Souperman with a grin. 'You'll be all right.'

'Thanks for saving me,' I replied. 'But you're still a phoney. The real Superman can fly.'

'I can fly,' he told me, 'but I couldn't get the can of soup open. When you rushed out of my flat you took something of mine with you. Look in your pocket.'

I felt in my pocket and pulled out a hard object. It was a bright blue can-opener.

ABOUT THE AUTHORS

ALEESAH DARLISON writes picture books and novels for boys and girls of all ages. Her story themes include courage, understanding, anti-bullying, self-belief, friendship and teamwork. Aleesah's picture books are *Little Meerkat*, *Bearly There*, *Puggle's Problem* and *Warambi*. Her chapter books include *Fangs* and *Little Good Wolf*. Her novels and popular series are *I Dare You*, the Unicorn Riders series, the Totally Twins series and the Ash Rover series. When Aleesah isn't creating entertaining and enchanting stories for children, she's usually looking after her four energetic children and her frisky dog, Floyd. Her website is www.aleesahdarlison.com

It has long been rumoured that **BILL CONDON** is a vampire or a werewolf. The truth is that he just looks like a monster because he is very old. He is so old that even his wrinkles have wrinkles! However, he still manages to keep feeling young by writing stories. That never fails to make him happy. In 2010 he won the Prime Minister's Literary Award for young adult fiction. Bill's latest novel, for junior readers, is *The Simple Things*, published in 2014. He lives on the south coast of New South Wales with his wife, the well-known children's author, Dianne Bates. Visit Bill at his website www.enterprisingwords.com.au

When **C. N. ARCHER** was a young girl, she dreamed of being an artist, an astronaut or an acrobat. Unfortunately, as it turned out, none of these occupations were particularly practical given she has very little artistic ability, suffers from terrible motion sickness and is as coordinated as a three-legged goat. Instead, she became a writer and dreams up stories about adorable trolls, evil fairies and glitter-farting unicorns. When she isn't writing, she enjoys playing board games with her husband and pets – a miniature dachshund and a Himalayan cat.

CLAIRE CRAIG wanted to be an archaeologist when she grew up but she became a book editor instead. Her first job was at the literary magazine *Granta* in the United Kingdom, where she had a crash course in 'who's who' in the literary fiction world. She then worked at many of the major publishing houses in Australia before realising her true passion for children's books. She wrote several non-fiction titles for children and some fiction readers for non-native speakers of English before she began writing stories about a nine-year-old girl called Harriet Bright who wanted to be a poet when she grew up. Under the pseudonym Petra James, Claire has also written the seven-book series ARKIE SPARKLE: Treasure Hunter. You can visit Harriet Bright's website at www.harrietbright.com

GEORGE IVANOFF is an author and stay-at-home dad residing in Melbourne. He has written over 70 books for children and teenagers, and is best known for his You Choose interactive books and Gamers novels. He has books on both the Victorian and NSW Premier's Reading Challenge lists, and he has won a couple of awards that no one has heard of. George has also had stories published in numerous magazines and anthologies, including *Trust Me Too*, *Stories for Girls* and *Stories for Boys*. George drinks too much coffee, eats too much chocolate and watches too much *Doctor Who*. If you'd like to find out more about George and his writing, check out his website: www.georgeivanoff.com.au

JANE JOLLY is a writer and teacher. Jane taught at Koonibba Aboriginal School and in 1983 she worked as a governess on Commonwealth Hill Station. Her award-winning picture books are: *Limpopo Lullaby*, a 2005 CBCA Notable Book; *Glass Tears*, a 2006 CBCA Notable Book; and *Ali the Bold Heart* (illustrated by Elise Hurst), a 2007 CBCA Notable Book. She has a large organic fruit and veg garden and loves eating the fresh produce from it. And she loves eating – especially chocolate. She also loves her chooks and their big brown eggs. She eats the eggs but never the chooks. You can visit Jane at www.janejolly.com

LIZZIE HORNE was born in Tasmania, but has lived in America, France, Perth, Sydney, Armidale and Melbourne. After moving what feels like a million times, she is happy to be back in country New South Wales, where she'd like to stay put for a while – when she's not travelling around the world! Lizzie has worked as a TV reporter, copywriter and creative director, speechwriter, poet, actor, bookseller, arts educator and mask-maker, and has her own range of greeting cards. She has a Bachelor of Languages and is also a mum.

R. A. SPRATT is an award-winning author and television writer. She lives in Bowral with her husband and two daughters. Her bestselling Nanny Piggins series stars the world's most glamorous pig, who also happens to be a chocolate-loving nanny. And like the heroine of her latest series, Friday Barnes, she enjoys wearing a silly hat. Spratt has two chickens and five goldfish, and her next-door-neighbour's cat thinks it lives in her house. For more information, visit www.raspratt.com

SALLY GOULD, a former lawyer, now writes for children up to 13 years old. *Fitness Fanatics* is her first story for Random House Australia. Her oldest son initially found reading difficult, which inspired her to write for boys who are reluctant readers. The antics of Sally's sons, one of whom is responsible and logical, and the other who is determined to have fun, inspire many of her stories. She lives in Melbourne with her husband, two sons and their two dogs.

PAUL JENNINGS, one of Australia's bestselling children's authors, was born in England and nowadays lives in Warrnambool, by the sea. *Unreal!*, published in 1985, was his first collection of stories for young people, and *The Gizmo*, published in 1994, was his first novel. In 1992 he became the first author to sell a million books in Australia. Although he is famed throughout the world for his accessible yet powerful short stories, he has also written picture books, novels and screenplays. The TV series *Round the Twist*, based on a collection of his stories, was a runaway success around the world and he won the Australian Writers' Guild Award for his screenplay. In 1998, he teamed up with another of Australia's bestselling writers for children, Morris Gleitzman, to create Wicked! and Deadly! — two gripping series of short novels. A recent book series is Don't Look Now, with cartoonist Andrew Weldon. For more information, visit Paul at www.pauljennings.com.au

ABOUT
THE EDITOR

Linsay Knight is widely respected as a leading expert in, and contributor to, children's literature in Australia. As former Head of Children's Books at Random House Australia, she nurtured the talent of numerous authors and illustrators to create some of Australia's most successful children's books. Linsay is also a lexicographer, having written and edited many dictionaries and thesauruses, is the author of a number of successful non-fiction books for children and adults, and the editor of a number of story collections, including *30 Australian Stories for Children*, *30 Australian Ghost Stories for Children* and two series of age-story collections like this one.

ABOUT THE ILLUSTRATOR

Tom Jellett has illustrated a number of books for children, including *Australia at the Beach* by Max Fatchen, The Littlest Pirate series by Sherryl Clark for Penguin Books, *The Gobbledygook is Eating a Book* by Justine Clarke and Arthur Baysting, *My Dad Thinks He's Funny* by Katrina Germein and the follow up *My Dad Still Thinks He's Funny* for Walker Books. Tom has also been included in the Editorial and Book category for the Society of Illustrators Annual Exhibition, New York in 2013 and 2014. He was also included in Communication Arts Illustration Annual 2012, 3×3 Children's Show No. 9, 10 and 11, and was Highly Commended in the 2013 Illustrators Australia Awards. For more information about Tom and his work visit www.tomjellett.com

ACKNOWLEDGEMENTS

'A Different Sort of Kelpie' by Aleesah Darlison first published in *The School Magazine*, February 2012. Text copyright © Aleesah Darlison 2014.

'The Big Bad Bah!' by Bill Condon first published by Random House Australia in 2014. Text copyright © Bill Condon 2014.

'Herbert Huffington: Tea-leaf Reader Extraordinaire' by C. N. Archer first published by Random House Australia in 2014. Text copyright © C. N. Archer 2014.

'Harriet Bright and the Very Big Fright' from *Harriet Bright in a Pickle* by Claire Craig first published by Pan Macmillan Australia in 2008. Text copyright © Claire Craig 2008.

'Liquid Mouse' by George Ivanoff first published by Random House Australia in 2014. Text copyright © George Ivanoff 2014.

'Rams vs Magpies' by Jane Jolly first published by Random House Australia in 2014. Text copyright © Jane Jolly 2014.

LOOK OUT FOR THESE OTHER GREAT STORY COLLECTIONS

OUT NOW